# To Be *Frank* and *Earnest*

## BY DAVID K. MEYERS

9/2/2021

**DORRANCE**
PUBLISHING CO
EST. 1920
PITTSBURGH, PENNSYLVANIA 15238

Dorrance Publishing Co
585 Alpha Drive
Suite 103
Pittsburgh, PA 15238
Visit our website at *www.dorrancebookstore.com*

ISBN: 978-1-6366-1402-1
eISBN: 978-1-6366-1978-1

# CONTENTS

# ACKNOWLEDGMENTS

First, I want to thank my late mother and grandmother for passing down the stories surrounding our family history that is the true inspiration for this book. Mom, I am glad you made me listen.

I also must acknowledge the research done by both my brother, Eric Louis Bernard Meyers, and my niece, Sharon Mattie Revis-Green, that provided much of the factual material I used. Of course, I want to also thank my two other brothers, Earl and Michael Meyers, for signing off on this project. And of course, my late sister, Gayle Katherine Fan Meyers-Weerasekera, whose fun personality I took the liberty to use in my story.

I was somewhat reluctant to publish this book because much of the material is very personal. The fact is that I finished the first complete draft in 2012 and did not get up the nerve to publish until about eight years later.

My near lifelong friend Glenn Bouttè read it and encouraged me, as well as my former high school debate and forensics coach Larry Smith, who both provided me with some great feedback and suggestions that I incorporated into the final manuscript.

Two other good friends got a sneak preview and pushed me over the edge to finally make this public: Doug Morris and Dolores Amato. And thanks to my hiking partner, Dr. Catherine Mathis, who had to hear about my writing and publishing woes for the last ten years… sorry, Cathy. I thank you all, and everyone else who put up with me during the years of this process.

# INTRODUCTION

As far as we know, we do not get to choose who we are, or where we are injected into this world... the stage upon which we live such an infinitesimally short time in the reality that we call our life. What is certain is that where we come from is indeed, from where we came, and we all have choices that we make that alter the stage for our children, and really the next societal generations.

Thus, the stage of this story derives inspiration from the life of a woman named Mattie Burton Meyers, my late mother. In most ways, she was a very ordinary modern American woman, and in other ways she was extraordinary, even through the eyes of one who was not looking up to her as their mother. The reality is the story of her family is just as exciting, and just as boring as the person sitting next to you... or anyone else for that matter.

What is unusual is the tale of her ancestral family told during recent generations is to such a large degree documented. Mattie, an American woman of African-American descent, during the latter half of her eighties decided to publish a series of stories, *her memoirs*, she had written about her life's experiences and her stories, the tales told to her as she was growing up. A couple of years before I wrote this book, she asked me, her youngest son, to help her put her narratives into book form.

I really did not want to do it, but it was my mother, so I reluctantly agreed. Shortly after accepting the job, I began reading my mother's writings and I began to realize that this was going to be a little more thought evoking, and in fact, much more emotional than I had anticipated.

The thought that this was the right thing to do struck me when I read her story entitled "Good Times with Grandpa Jim" and found myself staring in fascination at an old, tattered photograph of my grandmother's family taken in the rural setting of their Society Hill, South Carolina, farm maybe about 1917, give or take a year. My teenaged grandmother and her younger sister were stunningly beautiful young women.

As I worked with enhancing and bringing out the old photograph in my computer, my great-grandfather, wearing a very worn suit jacket and tie, but still in the tattered work pants that he probably was wearing before his wife, Julia Mae, had likely called him away from his work to be in the photograph, became clearly visible.

My two great uncles are posed with the appearance of typical elementary school-aged children with a look of total boredom on their faces, possibly wondering how long they would have to sit perfectly still for what would seem to a child as endless seconds as the photographer exposed the old silver oxide photographic plates.

I found the detail in the old photograph fascinating. The ghost image of the edge of my grandmother's dress that was apparently being blown in the breeze during the long exposure, probably taken in front of some part of their farm home on a bright sunny day, captured my imagination. It had to be a warm day because the two boys are both dressed in short pants with no shoes.

That night as I lay in bed waiting for my dreams to take control, I found myself thinking about the pen/pencil and notebook I could clearly see in "Grandpa Jim's" breast jacket pocket, and the stories my grandmother would tell me about her father. How he was an educated man, a black man with a college degree at the turn of the century. The pen/pencil and notebook made sense... he could read and write.

I wondered why they would have spent what would have been a good amount of money in those days to have an apparent professional photographer come to their home and take this family photograph at their farm. The question that rolled through my mind was if the reason for the somber expressions in the picture was due to the photographer's instructions, or if there was something else, some underlying thought that was on their minds.

I remembered my grandmother from my early childhood. I remembered how she would tell me about the 'gov'ment' taking their farm in a legal dispute, sometime around 1917. Now here it was in my mother's stories, right alongside a court case my niece, Sharon Revis-Green, had run across fully documenting a South Carolina Supreme Court appeal detailing the decision that overturned the inheritance of my great-grandparents' family.

That is when I decided I would take inspiration from her stories and attempt to create a fictitious story based on the history my mom conveyed in her memoirs.

I started writing this book in about October of 2010, just after we finished publishing my mom's stories. Then in August 2011, my mother's brother, her only surviving sibling, died. Upon the death of my uncle, we saw a little more of his life that was at the very least, *different* from what we all knew of him. Some *"what if"* questions popped into my mind that set the final stage for me to complete this book.

My mother passed several years before I decided to publish this story. Although she saw the first three chapters, she never had a chance to read the entire manuscript.

Although the plot is fictional, the basis of this story come from the historical facts surrounding the history of my mother's family, the actions of her brother, and how it all might have affected a group of fictitious people. You will note that I tried to separate the facts from my made-up plot. You can decide if I was successful in telling a compelling and entertaining story based on the documented history.

# PROLOGUE

## The Journey Begins

"... Stood on the banks of Jordan one day,

to see the ship go sailing over.

I stood on the banks of Jordan, yes I did Lord,

to see the ship go by..."

*-Stood on the Banks of Jordan-*
*Reverend James Cleveland*

# CHAPTER 1

## Adline Tedder

On a bright cold February morning in Bend, Oregon, a tall and very impressive-looking young man named Frank Malloy sat with his mother in a corporate aviation lounge at the Bend City airport. A dusting of snow had fallen the night before, and the mountains to the west reminded Frank of a picture postcard. To Frank, the black wet runways contrasted against the newly fallen white snow were equally beautiful.

At that moment, a man, one of the airport workers who apparently knew Frank, walked up to the pair and told them the airplane they were waiting to arrive had just started the approach into Bend, and should be on the ground in about five minutes. Frank said thank-you, and then quietly said something to his mother. She nodded and whispered a reply.

And five minutes later, the airplane, a shiny and very new, million-dollar single-engine turboprop taxied onto a parking place a few feet directly in front of the double glass doors that led out onto the airport's tarmac. Frank picked up both him and his mother's bags, along with the notebook computer he habitually carried, and together the two moved toward the doors.

About a minute after the airplane's propeller came to a stop, the air-stair door towards the back of the aircraft dropped down, and a fifty-year-old Black man named David Brewer, dressed in neatly pressed jeans, a short suede leather jacket, and scarf, stepped down and headed towards the door to meet Frank and his mother.

A few seconds later, an attractive Asian woman named Faye Brewer, also in jeans and wearing a black "STANFORD" hoodie sweatshirt, followed her husband off the airplane. She quickly pulled the hood-strings tight in the cold air, and then hurriedly walked over to meet the arriving fuel truck.

Less than ten minutes after landing, the airplane with all four people aboard was again airborne and quickly faded from sight into the southern Oregon sky.

This is really the *beginning of the end*... the end of a very bumpy journey for one of these individuals. You must understand that a little more than a year or so earlier, Frank Malloy thought he knew himself very well. This morning's trip is taking Frank and his entourage to explain why he was wrong. To know where they are going, or more importantly why, you need to start at the very beginning, and that beginning really starts at least one hundred and forty years earlier.

You see, it all really started on a hot and humid summer morning in Society Hill, South Carolina, with a young woman named Adline Tedder. In historical retrospect, Adline would still be amazed as to what she was experiencing on this bright morning in 1869. As the sound of roosters crowing in the warm predawn morning filled the air, her mind wandered over thoughts about being alive in a time that was so different from her past.

She realized that she had to hurry before her husband of three years would be coming in from his morning chores that included the ongoing repairs of their farm. The work made necessary from all the damages incurred before and during the "War Between the States" that ended just a few years earlier.

Amazed. One day she was a slave, one of more than thirty working on Master Bill and his wife's South Carolina plantation. Then today, well, today was quite different, really a world further from any dream she ever had when she was a little girl belonging to Miss Jimima and her family.

Looking back from her view on this early morning, while kneading the dough she would soon put into the fine iron stove to make her husband's favorite biscuits, her childhood appeared to have been a horror story existence, more horrible than any graveyard story Mama Mae had told when she was a child. However, as she ruminated about her childhood memories, she thought her life at that time was nothing outside of the ordinary, nothing bad... it was just her life.

"Lord knows it was jess normal," she uttered. "But the Lord delivers."

Adline thought about all the people she loved that did not make it to the *Promised Land* and she began to sing:

*"... Stood on the banks of Jordan one day, to see the ship go sailing over."*

Singing about the Lord made her feel so good and helped the time pass. As she sang, she thought of all the things she categorized as blessings. Her childhood was hard and fast, but it could have been much worse. She sang:

*"... I stood on the banks of Jordan, yes I did Lord, to see the ship go by..."*

She avoided a near-death sentence of working in the fields with most of the other Black slaves who were not as fortunate to be born with lighter skin color. This meant she would be more likely selected to work in the master's house.

Mama Mae had once told her that she was really the daughter of *Massa Griggs*, one of several offspring that stood right alongside their much darker brothers and sisters. She felt it was for that reason alone that she was delegated the task of being at first the playmate of Miss Jimima, and then later gaining a much better place in being part of the master's housework crew. Although this too was nothing outside of the normal, it was just her life.

Even as a child, Adline understood, like most slaves then knew, that there had always been a peculiar relationship between their White masters and the Black female slaves. To be sure, there was an unacceptable taboo of sex between a male slave and a White woman. So discouraged was the taboo that a violation would have resulted in the most terrible punishment for a White woman, and certainly death for the Black slave.

However, although uneducated, Adline was a highly intelligent woman who knew that anything that taboo begs for violations. She knew that violations often resulted in swift and fatal consequences, and without a doubt contributed to the myths about the sexual prowess of Black men that circulated among White southern women.

Back to reality, the cries of her young infant son awakening came right on schedule. Adline knew that she was going to have to get moving because the day was beginning in full.

By comparison, Adline and her husband were living a life that was far above the norm for the reconstructing South. They controlled about six hundred acres of prime farmland in Darlington County, about one-third of that acreage they by legal rights owned.

Adline and her husband were slowly rebuilding over the last couple of years because of destruction, damage and theft of the farm's property and implements during the War Between the States. Consequently, they now had a productive farm with decent crops and farm animals including cows to produce milk for their own consumption, as well as for resale to their neighbors around Society Hill.

The irony was that the cows that produced milk on the farm would have made the morning meal preparation much easier, by allowing her infant son to nurse from a milk-soaked cloth. However, Adline's infant son would go into near-death convulsions whenever she tried to feed him cow's milk in this manner. Thus, she knew she would have to stop and feed her son from her breast, and then let him play in his crib for the remaining time she was preparing the morning meal.

Adline also knew she would have to get her two older boys, who were just a couple years older than her infant, up and going for the day. Adline thought it better to wait until the last minute before bringing on that extra work on this morning.

However, her carefully choreographed routine factored in the task of feeding little Willie and getting Augustus and James up and dressed for the day. The biscuits were now cooking in the wood-fired iron stove her husband lit before he headed out that morning, alongside a big black pot of grits. She had thick slices of bacon ready for a frying pan, and she knew Minnie Griggs, her hired helper and former slave-time friend, would soon be coming in with the eggs and milk, and would help her finish her morning job… another amazement.

Ten years earlier, they were both slaves working for the wage of survival, and today, Minnie and her family were hired farmhands working for Adline and her husband for monetary pay.

Adline walked across the combination kitchen and eating area to the crib like bed her husband had made for little Willie when he was born a few months earlier. Little Willie expressed a cry of joy in anticipation of his mother's milk-laden breast, and then heartily started to nurse.

Adline cooed, "… Hush, child." She began to hum the same spiritual she was singing earlier, and her mind picked back up on the thoughts about the strange relationship between slave women and White men.

In 1859, a year before the first shots of the Civil War were heard off the coast at Fort Sumter, South Carolina, Adline and her fellow slaves that had once belonged to Mary Griggs were combined through marriage into one working unit with the slaves from Master Bill's Plantation.

Within the institution of American Slavery, Adline along with every slave on every American plantation knew that when it came to sexual encounters between a White man and a Black slave, everything was not only open to exploitation, but these sexual deviations were also in fact encouraged.

One should clearly understand that in the South, as with everywhere else in America, this was a White man's world. Treatment of women in the American States was as property. Thus, women had virtually no rights.

For instance, a woman who initiated a divorce proceeding would likely get nothing, including even being granted the divorce, if it were protested in any way by the defendant White husband.

However, White women were not on the same level as a farm animal. Consequently, moral practices about sex between a White man and his wife were firmly ground into the fabric of the southern lifestyle from both Biblical lessons, and the general prevailing sexual attitudes of the times. No such moral values existed for the Black slaves. For all practical purposes, Black slaves were farm animals.

As Adline's thoughts digressed to the year before the Civil War, she remembered her survival lessons from early childhood as they related to the deviant sexual behaviors of White slave owners. If the White master wanted to have sex with a young slave boy, there was nothing to stop him. Although this did not happen in her specific experiences, the stories she heard from other plantations said that it did, as well as other transgressions that she knew would "… make the Lord cry." She quietly sang:

*"… I stood on the banks of Jordan, yes I did Lord, to see the ship go by…"*

For the most part, from the myopic viewpoint of the White plantation owners, they tended to see themselves as privileged intellectuals involved in improving their holdings, along with the overall economic system. You might even say they saw themselves as agricultural scientists, experimenting with their ideas of eugenics.

In what we may now see as an epitome of arrogance, they saw themselves as merely improving their stock in much the same way as one would breed a prize bull with a herd of good Hereford cows. There was no downside. The slave owner typically ended up with more slaves, which meant more wealth, a win-win scenario that even today we would not question the motivational rationale. If they happened to enjoy their work, well, that was the benefit of privilege.

This practice probably led to the dichotomy between lighter- and darker-skinned slaves that even still exist today within both the American culture and African-American subcultures. One might think that the White slave-owners felt more comfortable and maybe even less threatened by those that looked more like them and showed signs of their common procreation.

Hence, those that they needed to be close to the house tended to be those lighter-skinned slaves like Adline, and with that closer contact may have been less subject to the harsh treatment and abuse of those who toiled in the fields and were less seen. Which one would you want to be?

Adline remembered her first sexual encounter with *"Massa Bill,"* the year before the War Between the States with serendipitous feelings. At thirteen years old, Adline was not the only slave girl to have been the recipient of Master Bill's desires, and at the time, she was sure that she would not be the last. Everyone in the house knew that Miss Jimima and he were not very intimate, and the years since the last of their children were born, they were not intimate at all.

The reasons for this lack of marital intimacy were not clear to Adline. Her Mama Mae used to tell her that Miss Jimima's marriage to Master Bill "… was somethin' that was set up by dem peoples yeas ago."

Then after Miss Jimima's last child was born, Jimima started taking to the sick bed, sometimes for days on end. And it was during that time period, Adline began sharing Master Bill's bed on a more regular basis, and soon found she was the only woman with whom the slave-master showed any sexual intimacy, a fact that was not missed by the other slaves, or for that matter, not missed by Master Bill's and Miss Jimima's common children.

Miss Jimima died in 1861, and Master Bill seemed to have no interest in seeking a new wife, instead choosing to continue to have his sexual desires fulfilled by his slave girl Adline.

Adline indeed had very mixed thoughts about this *relationship*. On one hand, the choice to become Master Bill's concubine was not hers. *Massa Bill* simply took her, she remembered, something no woman regardless of her social stature would want.

On the other hand, each time she subsequently shared his bed, she felt that much more protected from the harsh realities of a life in American slavery with all the real and implied consequences. Adline's primary thought at the time was the same goal that sat center in just about every slave's mind… to survive.

Adline would be a bit surprised to know that the feelings that rolled through her mind about her relationship with Master Bill was more common than she would have ever imagined, then or now. Adline had no doubts as to what she was to Master Bill… a piece of property for him to use at will.

Like a clock striking the top of the hour, Adline heard the back-porch door open, and smelled the aromatic blast of warm humid farm air sweep through the house.

"Good moanin', Miss Adline," said Big Jack as he passed her with a bushel of fresh corn he sat in a corner of the room.

The "Big" part of Big Jack's name was because he was a big and tall dark-skinned Black man. He was also Minnie's husband, and father of their four children.

As Big Jack passed his wife, he said a much quieter "Good moanin'."

Adline wiped Little Willie's face, and then put into his tiny hands, the toy horse that her husband had whittled from a wooden stick. Little Willie, now full and content as any infant is after a meal fresh from his mother, started playing with the toy horse, fingering and tasting the toy as Adline got up to finish off breakfast.

"Good moanin', Big Jack. Whatcha brang me this moanin'? Looks likes some fresh coan for suppa," said Adline.

Big Jack just replied, "Yes, ma'am. I gots da get them kids cleaned up for breakfast, Miss Adline," and headed back out the door.

While Adline was daydreaming and breastfeeding Little Willie, Minnie had pretty much finished off breakfast by frying the bacon, and putting the fresh milk into pitchers, and was now frying up some eggs, sunny side up, the way they all liked them.

"You go an' git dem boys up, Minne. I gots da rest now," Adline said to Minnie.

While Minnie went to get Adline's two older boys up, Adline walked over to the stove to give the grits a good stir before she took them off the fire and started placing the food on the table.

Big Jack came back in through the back door, this time with his four boys following, dirty, smiling, and ready to eat after doing their morning chores. They began to sit down. Even though they lived in a separate house on the farm, everyone, family and help alike, ate breakfast as a group, with the shared common goal of taking care of the farm. You might even say it was the morning staff meeting.

As they seated themselves around the large wooden kitchen table, a tall White man in coveralls walked into the kitchen with an air of ownership. He pulled out the chair at the head of the table, sat down, and immediately bowed his head. "Thank you, Lord, for this food…" He continued. "The Lord is my Shepherd, I shall not want, he maketh me…"

As William Tedder said "Amen," his wife proudly looked into the eyes of her husband, the man she once called *Massa Bill*, and began to serve his breakfast first.

Like any day, this was the start of another full workday, and another day of life for the Tedder family on their farm.

# CHAPTER 2

## William Tedder

Someone would likely describe William Tedder either as "*... his own man who is not afraid to think outside the box,*" or, "*... that crazy piece of White trash who lives down yonder with his nigger family.*" Either way, it is certain that William Tedder did at least one thing that was quite different from the post slavery status quo.

This specific Saturday morning in September of 1883 started as a near perfect day on the Tedder's farm. The summer seemed to finally be ending. Overnight the temperature had dropped, and it seemed to feel a little less humid as William and his wife Adline started another day on the farm. It was a little breezy that morning, which made the morning feel even better.

As usual, Adline was the first up and out doing her morning ritual of collecting chicken eggs at the crack of dawn when William came upon her outside the house.

"Good moanin', Adline," greeted William.

"Moanin'," Adline replied. Then in a louder voice, she said, "Mista Bill, I wants ya to kill dat uglay roosta and gets him ready for da pot. I declare, I'm tarred of dat roosta pesstin' me evrey day I go outs to gets my eggs!"

William laughed the way he always did when Adline talked about the big rooster that looked to be stalking her as he moved back and forth on the roof's edge above her head. "Now you know we can't kill that roosta, Adline. Mr. Roosta keeps them hens happy and making all them eggs every day," said William.

"I'll wrang that roosta's neck myself if'n he don't stop pesstin' me. Stew 'em all day with some dumplins for Saturday evenin' suppa," Adline remarked that got them both laughing.

Adline continued. "You still gots da rheumatism dis moanin', Mister Bill?" Adline put down her egg basket and walked over behind William and started rubbing his shoulder.

As Adline massaged his shoulder with her breast lightly touching against his back, William replied, "Well, it feels better now, Adline." There was still spark in his marriage to his much younger and still beautiful wife. Their relationship was still very much alive even after being together for more than 20 years.

"Where's Gus?" William asked, changing the subject. "You seen him this moanin'?"

"Gus was up foe me," answered Adline. "He be already down yonda workin' dem stumps you acts him 'bout." Adline lightly kissed the back of William's neck and then picked up her egg basket to return to gathering her eggs.

"I best to get to gettin' and get that boy workin' that stump foe breakfast," said William. "I still needs to get some time to get down to Darlington and start taking care of these kids and this land. Mayhaps later this week coming."

"An Mista Bill," Adline continued in a near command, "I needs you to be sho you gets the battub an heps me boil some watta so I can get me a batt in some Epson Saltz afta breakfast. Make sho you and yo boys gets a batt today too. Don't want any yo boys be stankin' at church tomarra... hea?"

"Me and Gus be seein' you for breakfast in an hour, an I will gets your bath, Miss Adline," as William turned to leave. "Lord have Mercy," he said in a lowered voice as he walked away.

"Alright, Mista Bill. This gonna be a glorious day, thanks da Lord," she loudly said as William left.

As William made the walk back through a treed area adjacent to his farm home, a thought occurred that sometimes, an arthritis flare-up in his shoulder would occur the day before it rained. But William concluded that could not happen today under such a beautiful cloudless morning sky such as today's. He was more concerned about an even bigger storm looming on the horizon that had nothing to do with the weather.

Although a rather quiet man, in recent years he found himself increasingly in the company of his present family, and their friends, and increasingly estranged from his own brothers, sisters, and his adult White children from years earlier. He had to say when he thought honestly about it, the entire divisive situation bothered him. However, he also acknowledged being a bit responsible for the present circumstance.

Just a few weeks previous, William had seen his own brother, Leonard, and his nephew in a local store, and they would not say hello to him. For several years now, the very church that he was born and raised talked of expunging him from their membership roster, because of his "immoral" marriage. For William, the latter situation wore hard on him because William saw himself as a God-fearing, Jesus-loving Christian, a feeling also shared by the rest of his current family.

And to add to the circumstance, Aunt Mary, his deceased wife's aunt, had died a few years earlier, and upon her death, Jimima's White daughter Mahalie and her husband had challenged parts of the will and legal agreement that had left William with the property rights of one-third of the entire estate. As William thought about it, the arrangement he made with Aunt Mary was indeed good for him and really for both his White and Black families, because it had saved the farm.

However, the entire business matter from the will of Mary's late husband William Griggs, and his subsequent business agreement with Aunt Mary was creating a tension that was bound to tear the two families completely apart. At this point, they, his White children, were acting just like the rest of the good White folk toward him and his Black children.

All the anger that was seemingly directed at him and his family from his community somewhat perplexed William because he saw most Whites living in the post-Civil War South as mainly concerned with getting on with their lives. To William, getting on with one's life meant accepting the status quo, and doing what was necessary to live within the new ways of doing things.

As with the outcome of many wars, most people who lived with a war in their own backyards became war weary and welcomed the end of the killing and destruction. Most accepted the consequences of losing and mainly sought to get on with what was left of their lives. It was no different when the Civil War ended. In the first two or three years following the end of the war, it appeared one of those realities was that former slaves were going to play a major role in southern politics.

However, William knew there were many Southern Whites who vowed to never accept the consequences of losing the Civil War and would do all that was required to reinstate some semblance of the former system. As William recalled, immediately following the end of the Civil War, the South Carolina legislature had drafted and passed a new constitution that essentially kept the newly emancipated slaves in the same subservient roles as they were under slavery, except they no longer referred to them as *slaves*.

You should clearly see that William was most definitely born and raised with privilege. His parents were both property and business owners. Being of such privilege he was schooled and had taken his place of privilege within the community he lived.

William and the other former citizens of the Confederate States of America may have been relieved to hear that President Abraham Lincoln had set the course for reinstatement of the Confederate States. That course set by President Lincoln allowed the former Confederate people to reestablish United States citizenship without imposing the most severe punishment many of his fellow Republicans wanted.

The first Military Reconstruction Act that was enacted by the United States Congress essentially said the new South Carolina constitution was not acceptable for reinstatement into the United States. The following year, South Carolina adopted a new constitution that was satisfactory to the Union. Among other things, it granted voting rights to former slaves.

Then there was the anger. Anger directed at the United States Government because they had imposed what the former slave masters viewed as harsh treatment of the former Confederacy. The former rebels also directed anger at themselves for the decisions that had led to their own demise. Mostly, there was anger directed at the former slaves, who for several years during Reconstruction were in legislative control of South Carolina.

William stopped, and looked out over a field that had been harvested a couple of months earlier, and let out a sarcastic laugh, and then said aloud, "How foolish."

How foolish, William thought, even how stupid some of these White people had been to think that former slaves when granted "freedom" were going to embrace their former masters. This group really believed that they had treated their slaves so well that the former slaves would want to be subservient, taken care of by the old slave owners.

William knew better because he had a little more insight into how the former slaves were thinking at the time. Turns out that William and his present wife had a well-functioning relationship that went back before the war. William had been alone for most of the years during the war. His previous wife had died just after the start of the Civil War, and his children from that marriage had all long left his household, except for his daughter Mahalie and her husband.

When William began to have sexual relations with Adline in the late 1850s, neither he nor other free White men saw anything wrong with what he and Adline were doing. That is, so long as William and Adline carried on quietly. The only difference was that being alone after his wife had died, he found himself actually *talking* with the slave girl Adline with whom he was sharing his bed, and maybe more important, listening to her talk about her feelings and dreams.

Thus, by listening to Adline, he knew that her dream of *freedom* did not mean a continuation of some manifestation of slavery. Adline also would tell him the visions of the freedom she expressed were representative of many, if not most, former slaves. Consequently, William knew that the notion of former slaves wanting to carry on a master/slave relationship was just pure stupidity.

To be sure, William would acknowledge that one of the main reasons he decided to start a family with Adline, and live with her as his wife had a lot to do with hanging onto his farm and business interest, in what he saw as the wave of possible reality in post-Civil War South Carolina. However, William would also tell you that by the time he set up housekeeping with Adline as a husband and wife following the war, he was also very much in love with her.

So much so that he asked his daughter Mahalie and her husband, who were living in his home, to leave, and the next day moved Adline into the home to live with him as his wife. This realization he knew was when the stress between him and his White children kicked into high gear.

It was one thing to use a slave or former slave for sex, and entirely something different when it came to being in any kind of public relationship. As his common-law marriage to Adline became public, the tension in both the community and his White family increased exponentially.

The fact was that neither his White family, nor the community could do a damn thing about it. He was in full control of the farm with a legally binding agreement between him and Aunt Mary. His White children could either play along with the program or leave the table.

As the area being worked by Gus came into view, he could see his oldest son Augustus working on removing a stump in an area where William was planning to add more hog pens during the winter. As he watched his oldest son Augustus struggling with the old tree stump, he realized how much he not only loved his children, but how well he liked his boys, especially his three oldest.

"You workin' that stump, or is that stump workin' you, Gus?" William asked the question with a big knowing grin as he approached his son.

His son Gus had a knack for figuring things out. That night before, William had told Gus to get started pulling out that old stump, and he would come and help him finish. He very purposely did not tell Gus specifically how to get the stump pulled out of the ground.

"Naw, Daddy, I don't think I need much more hep. I just about got it up."

Sure enough, nearly four hours after starting earlier that morning, Gus just about had that stump up and out of the ground. He could see how his son had the old work nag connected to a rope that tied around the stump. He saw how Gus had dug out around the stump and cut some of the roots. Very well done, William thought.

"Yeah, boy, I can see that," William replied as he examined with pride the method in which his oldest had attacked the problem. Although a very smart and strong boy, Gus was still a boy of 14 years old. His oldest son was just starting to develop the upper-body strength of the man he was becoming. However, William could see that if he gave Gus a little more time, he would get the roots cut and have the stump pulled out. However, he thought that enough time might be a couple of more days, and William wanted to have that stump out today. Besides, they needed to get back to the house for breakfast in a few more minutes.

So, William reached down and picked up the axe and said to his son, "But we ain't got until the second comin' to get that stump out, Gus. Lemme see what I can do."

As Gus stood back, William swung the axe up over his head and brought it down with all the strength he could focus out of his more than fifty-year-old body. That first swing of the axe sent some pain jolting through his arthritic shoulder.

William was a man accustomed to a lifetime of hard physical work that a farm life demanded. However, he had not swung an axe in a few months, and his first swing missed squarely hitting the root, and landed with a thud in the dirt.

His son, laughing, said to his father, "Daddy, I was doin' better than that!"

William, doing all he could to suppress his own laugh of embarrassment, looked at his son in mock anger and yelled, "Boy, you better get to gittin' the other side dug out so we can get this stump up before your brothers get up this morning, lest you be doin' all the cleanup too."

They both laughed as William swung the axe down with another powerful blow, this time hitting with a solid whack, completely cutting one big root. At his age, William knew how to pace himself to get the work done. In fact, the more he swung the axe, the better his shoulder felt.

William had never been a gentleman plantation owner like his father or his previous wife's uncle. He had always had the modestly sized farm where he worked right alongside the farm hands. Up until the end of the Civil War, he rented slaves when needed, and now, he hired free men that he paid wages.

He would swing the axe with all his strength for ten or so minutes and then tell Gus to clear out the trash, allowing himself a break for several minutes, and then swing the axe some more for a few more minutes.

William had another trick for getting hard work done. He just did not think about the work, instead letting his thoughts wander. As he swung the axe, he thought. At his age, he was pretty much an old man in this time when most men seldom lived past age fifty. His oldest son was now an educated young man, having successfully completed the sixth grade, the highest grade level available for most Black people at the time. Public education for Blacks was also new, a product of the post-Civil War constitution in South Carolina.

William thought, as he had planned over the years, Gus was now working full time on the family farm. William could see that in a few more years, Gus working at his side would have both the physical strength, and mental tools required to manage most of the actual work on the farm.

With Gus' younger brother James finishing sixth grade next year, William figured with a little experience both of his boys ought to give him a little breathing space in three or four years. Although William thought that James who had a lot of his mother in him, especially when it came to the Lord, might want a little more than a life on the farm.

William and his son together worked on the old stump for about an hour, until William could see that Augustus would be able to haul the stump out of the area they were clearing. He said to his son, "You and your brothers, get that stump and all that trash out of here before you come to dinner. You hea?"

"Yeah, Daddy," replied Augustus.

"Now, let's get back to the house for breakfast, boy," suggested William. "You gets the rest of that stump done after breakfast, you hea?"

Then, William and Augustus walked back to the house to have their breakfast with the rest of the family.

William would often think about how things had changed for not just him, but the entire world he lived since birth. It seemed like the thirty years that had passed since the beginning of the Civil War was like going to the moon. His children, the sons and daughters of a former slave, were going to school directly resulting from legislation adopted at the end of the war.

He thought how different his life had diverged from before the death of his previous wife in 1861. His first thought was that he had lived a much happier life since the death of his wife Jimima. William was proud of his accomplishments.

The deal he made with Jimima's Aunt Mary put William in control of the entire estate. More importantly, William running the operation had saved the entire estate. He sold slaves to pay off the debt and get the farm out of foreclosure, and then he used the rest of the money to restock and replant the farm.

By the end of the war things were working very well for all the Tedders. Except, his White children now had some issue with him, not even a blood Griggs, being in line to receive such a large share of the estate when Mary died. His daughter Mahalie and her husband unsuccessfully challenged the property distribution following Mary's death.

He was not happy with the children from his previous marriage, primarily because they really sided with his daughter and her husband to limit his inheritance. He understood that his other White children would have also challenged the will along with Mahalie, if they had not been afraid of losing their shares of the two-thirds of Aunt Mary's estate the original will legally provided to the heirs after her death.

Surely, their muted objections had as much to do with the marriage to his present wife Adline and their Black family. Mainly, he believed it had all to do with plain old greed. He had to admit that he had a problem with that.

However, today William was more concerned with the not-so-good changes he saw coming that extended far beyond this internal family feud. This bigger change had to do with the present sociopolitical climate in South Carolina, the South in general, and for that matter, the entire country.

For several years after the end of the Civil War, the former slaves ran the South Carolina legislature. At one time, African-Americans filled almost three-fourths of the legislative seats. When Federal Troops were in the South to enforce the laws, things were not too bad for the newly emancipated slaves.

However, almost immediately, the number of Federal troops each year dwindled in numbers, and this allowed a fertile environment for the eruption of groups such as the Ku Klux Klan to flourish. As the troops dwindled, these groups increasingly terrorized Blacks to keep them away from the polls. Today in 1883, things were quite different.

William loved his children, especially his four older Black boys, and knew he had to do as much as possible to seal their future against the changing South.

That evening after dinner, William sat down with the three oldest boys, Augustus, James, and Willie, and first started talking about what tasks were pending for the next day. He began by asking Gus about how far along he was on the tree stump project.

Gus spoke. "Daddy, I got that stump up out of the middle of the yard. That's the last one. Willie and Samuel helped me get the trash into a big pile, so we can burn it up in the mornin'."

His father laughed. "Boy, you think you gonna get all them fresh green stumps to burn?"

"Naw, Daddy. That's why I put it 'top all that old trash from last year to get started good and hot," his son explained.

"You did real good, Gus. I want you and Big Jack to start splittin' them logs from last winter so we can use them for fence post by this next spring comin'. I figure that will take the two of you a couple of weeks or more."

William went on explaining what he wanted done. "I been tellin' you kids we gonna add some more space so we can pen about two or three times as many hogs down yonder where Gus and I cleared them old trees. I surely would likes to get them new hogs in them pens by spring."

William paused and then continued speaking in a slightly different tone.

"There's something else. The other reason I want to talk with all you boys before you get to bed is 'cause I got the newspaper from Charleston when I was in town yesterday. Now there seems to be a lot of talk about how things are changing for coloreds after the election of this Rutherford Hayes president last year. It ain't like I thought it would be when you kids were born.

"I don't want any of you boys walkin' along at night at all. I don't even want you walkin' alone anytime if'n you can help it. I hear they hung a colored boy over in the other county for *lookin'* like he wanted to do somethin' to this White woman. Now mayhaps they is more to it. But you watch how you act, and who you talk to. Them days of the Union enforcin' the law is long past, and we are in dangerous times, boys."

William looked directly at James and said, "So, you boys do what I say. Especially you, James, and your brother Willie when you be walkin' to and from that school every day. You do stay together, and you watch out for strangers. You understand me, boy?" staring at James.

"Yeah, Daddy," replied both James and Willie.

James had a little more to say, and quickly added, "I saw Uncle Leonard when I was walkin' home. He told me to tell you he was gonna be plantin' the creek land in the spring."

"Boy," William spat out, "… you don't be studyin' no Leonard. You let me deal with your kin about that creek land. But I'll tell ya what, he ain't gonna be plantin' my creek land no time soon."

On that note, William prayed with his boys, and said goodnight. Sometime after William and his boys were all in bed sleeping, a late autumn storm blew in from the coast, a hurricane, releasing its fury over his little patch of South Carolina farmland. Seems that William should not have so quickly dismissed his intuitive thoughts of his arthritic shoulder earlier that morning.

William knew that all the plans he had just laid out for his boys to get done the following day would have to be changed after he surveyed the damage being done by all the wind and rain being unleashed out of the heavens. They certainly would not be burning that trash pile for quite some time considering the heavy rain presently falling.

William had no idea that the storm outdoors was nothing in comparison to the storm that would dog him and his boys for the next 22 years. Moreover, it would have been impossible for William to have the slightest inkling that the course he and Adline set before 1868 would be firmly in the minds of the four travelers who would board an airplane, 3,000 miles away, and more than one hundred and forty years later.

# FRANK'S RESEARCH

## *The Tedders*

It is accurate to conclude that Frank Malloy at the very least was intrigued when he first heard the story of the Tedders. But it was just a story. If it were a true story was the question that mostly intrigued him. Unfortunately, Frank could not just pick up the phone and make a call to someone who was dead for more than a hundred years.

However, Frank thought that maybe he could determine the story's plausibility by looking at as much factually documented information he could find regarding the tale he had heard. He started his research at first writing notes on a single sheet of unlined paper that would grow to several organized boxes of material in his small home office.

Verification of the information was Frank's first task when he began his research regarding the Tedder families. Thus, on a late November evening he sat at a glass-topped desk in front of a rather large computer screen, bathed with the glow of a soft fluorescent desk lamp.

He thought it was important that anyone be able to minimally go to a computer or the local library and get the same information he had used researching the Tedders. What factual clues Frank had to start with were the names of two court cases, *Moody v. Tedder* and *Tedder v. Tedder,* both cases he knew occurred in South Carolina.

He entered the words *"Moody v. Tedder"* and *"South Carolina"* including the quotation marks into the Google search engine and found a book reference for *Reports of Cases Heard and Determined by the Supreme Court of South Carolina, Volume 16,* with the full book published as a PDF document file. Starting on page 557, Frank read the court document.

*Moody v. Tedder* is the 1882 decision handed down by the South Carolina Supreme Court about an appeal regarding an inheritance dispute between Mahalie Moody and her father, William Tedder Jr. The primary significance to Frank at this point is that the court case verifies the existence of William and Jimima Tedder's White family and details the source of William's wealth. Frank found corroboration of the existence of the White family members in the form of United States Census records between 1820 and 1870 that he located through the "Ancestory.com" website.

Frank repeated the process for "*Tedder v. Tedder*" and found a similar book, *Reports of Cases Heard and Determined by the Supreme Court of South Carolina, Volume CVIII.* He found the specific 1917 court decision starting on page 271.

The court documents of both *Moody v. Tedder* and *Tedder v. Tedder* provide much detail about William and Jimima Tedder's family. Additionally, the cases verify the existence of William Tedder's second family who were African-American, and his marriage to the former slave, Adline. Succinctly, these two documents factually describe the history of the Tedder families. To start, they clearly say that Jimima was white, and her maiden name was Griggs.

First, Frank found through the *Moody v. Tedder* document that William and Jimima Tedder, and their White family are real historical people. Census records and court documents say William was born around 1821, in Society Hill (Antioch Township), South Carolina, to William and Phoebe Tedder who were "engaged in agriculture" according to the 1830 census. That same census record also lists a total of seven children in the William Tedder Sr. household. William Tedder Jr. was the youngest. William Tedder Jr. married Jimima, sometime in the early 1840s.

The court documents further state that Jimima was the niece of William and Mary Griggs. Prior to the Civil War, William and Mary Griggs owned a large farm, a plantation of about six hundred or so acres including many slaves. Jimima died about 1861 according to the court records.

*Moody v. Tedder* says William ended up with complete control of the entire estate starting in 1856, resulting from a legal arrangement made between him and his wife's Aunt Mary following the death of Mary's husband in 1851. When Mary died in 1873, *Moody v. Tedder* states that William Tedder received deed to approximately one-third of the former Griggs estate because of that legal agreement with the late Mary Griggs.

Frank laughed a little when he started to examine the 1917 case of *Tedder v. Tedder* because it depicted a second marital relationship with William Tedder and a former Black slave named Adline that at the very least started within a couple of years after the end of the Civil War. He did not laugh because of the mixed-race relationship. He laughed because William and Adline started a brand-new second family when William was well into his forties.

*That's certainly something I would not do*, thought Frank.

Frank determined that these were all the same people with a common family relationship. The *Tedder v. Tedder* court record in detail connects the relationships between them all. Additionally, *Tedder v. Tedder* contains information stating that Adline was originally the property of William and Mary Griggs.

The birthdate for Adline is either 1840 or 1844, depending if you use the 1880 census record or the information regarding Adline in *Tedder v. Tedder*. The imprecise birthdate for Adline is very consistent with slave-era record keeping. The information regarding Adline cited in *Tedder v. Tedder* unequivocally states that she was a former slave, originally the property of William and Mary Griggs, and then became the *personal* property of Jimima.

Testimony cited in *Tedder v. Tedder* says that right after the end of the Civil War, William and Adline began living together in the home that William previously occupied with his late wife Jimima. At the time of the 1880 census, Augustus, the oldest son of William and Adline was twelve, making his birth year to be in 1868, which implies his year of conception to be as early as 1867.

In the 1880 census, William Tedder Jr. listed four "sons" and one daughter. He entered Augustus' occupation as a "laborer." Additionally, William entered son James as age 11, Willie as age 7 and Samuel, the youngest son, on the record at age one. The census record uses the term mulatto to describe the four oldest children listed in the record. Frank also noted the school enrollment notation next to each of the four eldest children on the census document.

Frank observed that William entered Adline into the 1880 census as his *wife*, as well as claiming all four of his Black offspring as his "children." *Tedder v. Tedder* cites testimony by at least seven people who say William Tedder routinely and publicly acknowledged both his marriage to Adline, as well as his

Black children. There was no testimony that categorically said this family relationship was not common knowledge within the area they lived.

Frank found several other interesting facts gleaned from the court cases and census documents regarding William and Adline's family. The ongoing "marital" relationship between William and Adline began about 1867 and continued at least until Adline's death in 1890. In 1888, the last sibling, Katy, was born. This birthdate documentation comes from the 1900 census with Katy's age entered as 12 years old. William would have been about 67 years old at the time of Katy's birth.

From this information, Frank concluded that both William Tedder's Black and White families are historically real families. He concluded this family really did exist and Frank thought it was important that he document the source of his materials so others may be able to duplicate his findings. He made careful notes.

Of course, this information is largely irrelevant without knowing exactly who Frank Malloy is, and why he did this research in the first place.

# PART I

## Frank, Cheryl, and Fred

*"...she was there when I found her, and she was there when I lost my best friend... I may wade in still waters, but I'll never swim Kern River again."*

*- Merle Haggard*

# CHAPTER 3

## *Cheryl and Frank*

*If I can just get into the house without any direct contact with mom, I will be okay,* thought a teenaged Frank as he quietly pulled his keys out of his pocket on this specific evening.

If you were to have asked Franklin Malloy about his life's direction just a year before he and his mom departed the Bend airport on that cold February morning, he would have told you something altogether different. Up until then, Frank, even as a teenager, thought he knew the quintessential facts about who he was quite well.

Franklin was born 30 years earlier to an attractive White woman named Cheryl Malloy, who had moved to California's Sacramento Valley during the late 1970s. For a little less than four years, Cheryl lived in Sacramento, California, where she worked as a restaurant server until she became pregnant with Franklin, and then returned to Bend, Oregon, where Franklin was born. She never returned to Sacramento.

Cheryl grew up in the same Bend, Oregon, home where she was born and raised by her mother and now deceased father. Even now, the city of Bend is a small city of substantially less than 100,000 residents, nestled against the eastern side of the Cascade mountain range where the geography slopes off into the high desert of eastern Oregon.

For the first part of Franklin's life, he too lived in Bend with his mom in his grandmother's home. After Frank, as he was commonly called, started school in the mid-eighties, Cheryl took a job at a grocery store, and about the same time, enrolled in classes at the local community college.

Three years later, she earned an Associate of Arts degree in accounting and almost immediately went to work maintaining the books and doing payroll for a man who owned a truck stop on the outskirts of Bend.

When Frank was about ten years old, Cheryl's Aunt Marylyn, his grandmother's only sibling, died suddenly, leaving her home to Cheryl's mother. Frank, along with his mother, ended up living in their deceased aunt's home located in an older section of Bend. It was in this house that Franklin spent the rest of his childhood and early adult life.

By the time Frank was entering high school, it was apparent he was going to be a tall, strong, and impressive-looking young adult. He was already six feet tall, with wavy light brown hair and a smile that made you want to be around him.

He was well liked, and an above-average student. Although like many adolescents coming into their own, Frank went through a stage where he began to show an undercurrent of resentment and even a bit of anger toward authority, especially with his mother. As it turns out, he really did have a reason to be angry with his mom.

It was on the last day of Frank's junior year in high school when he came home from school, after hanging out with a couple of his friends, drinking beer and smoking marijuana up at the nearby Crater Lake.

So today, Frank's one thought as he put his key into the front door was to avoid any close physical contact with his mom as he walked in, because he knew she would not have any tolerance for either activity. It is funny how mothers always have a knack for discovering the things that their son's do wrong.

*Please, Mom. Please be in the back of the house and let me sneak into my room,* Frank thought as he slowly turned the key.

He would have been better off crawling in through his bedroom window. As bad luck would have it, his mother was picking up some old magazines that Frank himself had left carelessly tossed in a pile, right next to the front door before leaving home that morning. She was so close that Frank nearly hit her with the door as it opened.

Sure enough, after barely taking one breath, Cheryl said to her son, "You've been smoking marijuana, Frank!" Her tone of voice and the color of her face made it obvious to Frank that she was not happy in the least.

Frank tried to put a few steps between him and his mother as she was talking.

"How many times have I told you about that? I will not have you smoking marijuana or using any drugs while you live in this house, Franklin."

Cheryl kept her son cornered in the doorway as she continued. "Don't you want to graduate from high school, Frank? You know that stuff keeps you from getting any work done, especially your homework."

As Frank closed the door and tried to move past her in the cramped entryway, she caught a bit more of Frank's breath and continued, "... and you've been drinking too!"

Frank did what just about every other teenager would do. He denied and rationalized everything. "Mom, I have not been smoking pot. I just went up to the lake with Sara Jane, Ronald, and Ben when we got out today at noon. You know, last day of school, start the summer party? Ben was smoking pot, not Sara or me. I did drink a beer."

Cheryl thought this sounded plausible. Frank was not acting as if he was under the influence of anything other than her interrogation. She knew all the kids Frank had mentioned. Sara and Ronald were studious kids that she knew well, both them and their families. In fact, she had known both Sara and Ronald's parents when she was growing up in Bend. However, Ben Reynolds was altogether different. Her reply to Frank was in a somewhat conciliatory tone.

"That may be true, Frank, but just being with someone who is doing something illegal is enough to get you in trouble too. And Ben has a history of leaving you holding the goods."

Cheryl thought a moment before speaking. "I've got to tell you what I think, Frank. That Ben is just plain weird. Is he still playing with that Nazi junk?"

"Lighten up, Mom," Frank replied. "Half the time, I don't think Ben knows what he's doing himself."

The problem with Ben Reynolds was that earlier in the school year, he had become enthralled with the weaponry he found described at a neo-Nazi website. This kind of media along with the emergence of some violent paramilitary video games was a new phenomenon in the mid-nineties. Ben had become so caught up with it that he printed some of the Nazi literature and was suspended from school when he was caught passing it out a few months ago. Ben was also Frank's best friend going back to first grade.

"Ben just does stuff without thinking things all the way through sometimes," Frank added and then continued talking after taking a few steps around his mother. "That's why he gets caught doing the stupid stuff a lot of us do, Mom."

Cheryl replied, "You may be right about him. Although, I have to say that Ben Reynolds is one person I wish you would avoid. You'll end up in serious trouble if you keep hanging around him."

In defense of his friend, Frank said, "Ben is just trying to find somewhere that he thinks people will notice him, Mom. By the end of the summer, he'll be on to something else. He is still my best friend. But I'm not into any of that junk that he's into, Mom." Frank paused before he added, "I am not as impressionable as Ben, and I don't believe in any of that weird stuff."

"Well, maybe you aren't as impressionable, Franklin, but he's surely just got you in trouble again with me." She continued in a more conciliatory tone with a plea. "You know, I trust you, Franklin, but when you are not one hundred percent honest with me, you put a lot of strain on the trust I have with you. Are you being absolutely honest with me… about what you were doing at the lake?"

If Cheryl thought about the potential "can of worms" her comment may evoke, she would have never said the words that had just come out of her mouth.

Frank looked at his mother with eyes that could have lit a fire. He said in a monotone, "You mean the way you have been honest with me about my father?"

"Mister Malloy," Cheryl exploded. "You do not question why and what I may ask you! I am your mother and there are certain things you do not address to me as if I am *your* child."

"Well, Mom…," Frank blurted back and was cut off mid-sentence as his mother continued.

"You do not question me, Frank. You are sixteen years old and live under my roof. There is no democracy in this house. Anything I choose to tell, or not tell you are my decisions. Live with it!"

"That's what I mean, Mom," Frank went on in a softer voice. Trying to sound more levelheaded, he explained, "Mom, my last name is Malloy, your last name. My birth certificate says my father is someone named Fred Langton. You and Grandma have both said that is not true. I wish you would just tell me something. Anything as long as it is true. Is that so hard?"

Cheryl thought, the fact is that she had told her son some things about his father. Over the years, she had told him there was nothing wrong with his father. To her knowledge, Frank's father had never been in trouble with the law, worked an honest job for a living, and generally was a decent man. It was also true that Cheryl had once told Frank that "Langton" was not his father's actual last name, because she claimed she did not remember.

What she really intended was that she had no desire for Frank to meet up with his father at any point in the future if she could help it. The last thing she was going to do was give Frank his father's full name, period. She did tell him that the last she knew, Frank's father was living somewhere in California. Nevertheless, if she knew more, she was not telling that either.

She asked aloud, "Why is this so important to you, Franklin? I know it is hard, but these are the choices of your father. The important thing is that you have a family that loves you, Frank. I am being as honest with you as possible for everyone's good."

Frank's reply was very blunt. "Because he is my father and I deserve to know, and I don't think you're being honest with me."

The truth was Cheryl had a hard time just thinking about Frank's father because it brought back so many different emotions for her. In reality, Cheryl's mother had little more information than Frank. Over the years, Cheryl and her mother had more arguments on this subject than could be counted. Each argument would end the same way. Cheryl would just say to her mother, "I love Frank, and I want him to live a full life without any burdens that I have created."

So, on this evening, she ended the argument with Frank the same way she ended the discussions with her mother. She said, "Frank, I love you. However, the business between your father and me does not involve you, really, Frank. I promise I will tell you everything I know, at least that you need to know, when the time is right."

Frank sarcastically replied, "Sure, Mom. When will that be?"

"When I think it is the right time, and it is not right now." As she turned to walk away, Cheryl added as she was walking away, "By the way, consider yourself grounded for the rest of the week."

Frank thought at least today is Friday.

If you were to have asked Cheryl, she would have told you that she really wanted to tell Frank everything she knew right then. However, she did think that this was not a time to drag up the past consisting of what she termed as irrelevant stuff about Frank's father.

For the next year or so, Cheryl somewhat held up the promise to tell Frank more about his dad, although she would usually only volunteer small parts to Frank regarding his father at any specific time.

For instance, she told him that Fred was a truck driver, and at times worked as a cowboy with a special talent for training horses. She said his father was smart but lacked a formal education past sixth grade because he had run away from home as a child, and never went back to finish his education. She would often say to Frank that he looked like his father and had many of the same physical features.

However generally, the two never had any real in-depth discussions regarding Fred Langton. That is how it was until a few months after Frank had graduated from high school. On this specific day, Frank was telling his mom about something that happened earlier in the afternoon when he had seen one of his former teachers at the supermarket.

He was saying, "… it turns out that my teacher was really a preacher, without a single feature."

Frank was sitting at the dining table laughing hysterically as he would do when he just realized the humor he had created. His mother, leaning with her back braced against the kitchen counter, had a slight smile on her face as she tried to suppress her own laughter.

Suddenly, realizing the attention his mom had focused on him, Frank sensed that her stare had little to do with what he had specifically said. He stopped laughing. "Mom, why are you looking at me like that?"

Cheryl asked, "Where did you hear that?"

"I just made it up as I was talking. Mr. Thomas was definitely a *preacher teacher*, and never showed a frown or smile… totally featureless… you get it?" Frank said to his mom.

"No… no, I get it, Frank. That wasn't what caught my attention. When you were creating that little rhyme about your teacher, I had a realization. It occurred to me that who we are really is passed down through our parent's genes, more so than I previously thought." She paused and then continued. "I don't think I ever realized that to some extent, blood is a major factor in determining who we are, and maybe even how we act, until this very moment."

She continued, "I can see that you have a lot of your father in you, whether I have said that to you or not, Franklin." Cheryl tended to call him Franklin when she was consciously trying to speak to him on an adult level.

With a bit of a hysterical laugh, she added, "It just goes to show, we are destined to be who we are, no matter."

Frank again sensed there was something else on her mind and had an idea what it might involve. He leaned back a little in his chair, and forced himself to ask in a subdued tone, "Mom... just what is it that is so horrible about my father?"

Cheryl stopped leaning against the counter, stood up straight, and said, "Nothing... absolutely nothing. You have to believe that Franklin."

Then Cheryl walked over to the table, pulled out the chair directly across from Frank, and sat down. She made it a point to look directly into her son's eyes when she made the next statement.

"Frank," she said, "if you had every character attribute of your father, good, bad, and ugly, you would be an outstanding man. The simple fact is you do have many of those same character traits as your father. You have his sense of humor for one. And like I have told you before, you look just like him. That's a good thing," she added with a slight giggle.

Frank started to interrupt, but his mother held up a finger and said, "Let me finish telling you what I am about to tell you, Franklin."

Frank simply said, "Okay," and let his mom continue. He was not going to lose this opportunity to hear what sounded like some never revealed nuggets of information about his father.

"The first thing for you to know, Franklin, I was very much in love with your father," she said as she continued her story. "There was nothing wrong with your dad. He had two legs, two arms, and all of his fingers and toes." She laughed and added, "Fred had the most beautiful smile. He could make you laugh without even trying, just as you did a few minutes ago. He would take the simplest sentence and make it rhyme in a way that would make you laugh. He seemed to do it automatically, just like you. He's the type of man that when you know him, you just want to be around him."

Cheryl went back to a serious tone and said, "I am going to tell you as much as I can remember about your father right now, Frank. Anything that I tell you should not make or break your life. You have to believe me when I say that your life does not need to bear a burden that has nothing to do with who you are."

Cheryl thought for a moment before she continued. "I am also going to tell you some factual things about my life before I met your dad. I hope you do not judge me too harshly, but my early life had some very rough spots. The primary reason why I have not talked much on this subject is that I will have to tell you some things about me... what I have done that I am not proud in the least. You have to know that part about me, so you can understand the context... where I was at the time I met your dad."

"Well, Mom, why did...," Frank started to ask and was cut off by Cheryl.

"Do you want to hear this or not, Franklin?" She continued after a pause, "I honestly do not remember what Fred's real last name is because it has been too long ago," said Cheryl, appearing to choose her words carefully. "Nor do I have any idea exactly where he is presently living, although I would imagine he is still somewhere in California."

"I tried to find him a few years after you were born and could not locate him. He had long since moved from Sacramento."

She perked up and looked at Frank. "Sacramento... that's where we first met."

For the next two hours, Cheryl told Frank about her life. She told him how she met his father... an exceedingly long and detailed story. She told him everything she could think of about her past life, her relationship with Fred... and almost everything about Frank's father.

# CHAPTER 4

## Frank and Ernest

"I remember the day I met Fred perfectly," Cheryl said as she started telling her son the story about how she met Fred. "I was working at the Dew Drop Restaurant in Sacramento. It was in the middle of summer in 1982, I think. What I remember most was that sad song, 'Kern River' by Merle Haggard, playing on the radio." Cheryl laughed. "Fred caught my interest because he just stuck out."

Even though Merle Haggard composed the song after his dog drowned in the Kern River, when Fred heard this song in 1982, he was sitting in this restaurant thinking about how much he missed his mother, who had died nearly twenty years ago. He still missed her. It had nothing to do with a drowned dog in his mind.

Fred was sitting at the counter after just finishing his breakfast as he ruminated over the fresh feelings about his mother. It was really just a little diner with a well-worn 1950s-style counter, stools that had been patched a number of times, and a dated countertop showing the thirty years of service to an uncountable number of patrons.

There were a few booths and tables, but Fred always sat at the counter, always near the cash register, so he could talk to the waitresses, cooks, manager, patrons, or anyone else who had the time. Fred was a decent guy, but clearly a loner.

There was a jukebox next to a window overlooking the highway, but on a morning such as this, the radio was playing, tuned to the local KRAK-AM radio station so truckers could hear the local news and the two types of music most patrons of the Dew Drop thought was of any good, Country and Western.

This fit perfectly well with Fred. His "5X" Stetson hats, Tony Lama boots, and string tie worn with his western sports jacket seemed to fit his six-foot-four muscular body like a Hollywood cowboy star. In fact, he almost looked like a sibling of James Dean.

As rundown as it was, during the tomato-harvesting season this was a great little base of operations for a truck driver like Fred. There was a restaurant with decent food, a motel with clean rooms and cheap prices by the week, and a country and western bar featuring live music on the weekends.

Moreover, it was right along the old highway with a big open field behind the rooms where the truckers could park their rigs. Someone had even rigged up several water hoses long enough to reach their parked tomato-hauling trucks, a perfect solution for washing down the big white hauling bins rigged on top their flatbed trailers at the end of the day.

If there were any shortcomings about residence at the Dew Drop Motel Bar and Grill, it was the first stop for inmates just released from Folsom Prison a few miles up the road. However, the truckers and the ex-cons generally kept to their own groups. Although, the newly released jailbirds occasionally found themselves in the hire of the truckers, hosing out the trailers for a couple of bucks.

That shortcoming did not worry Fred to any degree. Fred had a knack for avoiding danger when in the presence of the dangerous. He developed his survival skills when he was a young runaway during the years of the Great Depression, riding the boxcars with a host of unsavory characters. At six feet four, he was big enough, and had a tough enough muscular appearance to inspire a second thought for most who might contemplate approaching Fred too aggressively.

Fred was both Frank and Earnest. As the old saying goes, Fred was Frank in Seattle, and Ernest in LA. Meaning, Fred had acquired some of the survival characteristics of a chameleon, in that he had a way of making his personality and presentation fit in with a specific individual or group. In short, a wide range of people tended to like Fred, from the most to least desirable.

Cheryl described that man to her son Frank. To be sure, Cheryl had her own baggage that she had taken to Sacramento. She said to her son, "Before I tell you exactly how I met Fred, I need to explain how I ended up running away from a very embarrassing self-imposed life. Frank, I had an unbelievably bad time for the first ten years after high school.

"When I moved to Sacramento, California, with my then friend Sally Jones, I was 28 years old and had absolutely no idea what I was going to do with my life.

"In contrast, my friend Sally, who had a five-year-old daughter at the time, actually had a pretty good plan to attend Cosumnes River Community College, and work for her second cousin at the Dew Drop Motel in North Sacramento. I think Sally was about twenty-five at the time. Sally's cousin had purchased the Dew Drop and the adjacent apartments from his family.

"You weren't born until after I left Sacramento," she said. "I was briefly married twice during the ten years I lived in Portland, thankfully, without any children. That was an extremely hard ten years. Ten years I would just as soon forget.

"You see, Frank, I left Mama's house in Bend a few days after my high school graduation in 1967, along with my then high school boyfriend, and moved to Portland, Oregon, against the best advice and pleas from Mama.

"Mama said she was depressed every day for the next ten years and cried for days when she would hear some of the bad news about my self-imposed lifestyle. To this day, I ask for her forgiveness just about every time I see her.

"But that was in 1967, Frank." Cheryl laughed slightly and added, "Sex, drugs, and rock and roll? That all sounded appealing to a couple of eighteen-year-old kids from a small rural community. Although Portland was not exactly San Francisco or LA, it was the big city in the view of a small-town Oregon girl like me, as well as my boyfriend. It was a very rebellious and adventurous time for anyone of my age."

Frank interrupted, with a tone of disbelief he asked, "You mean *you* were taking drugs?"

"Yes, I did. Marijuana and acid, or LSD," Cheryl answered. "Along with just about everyone I knew when I was in high school. There were many who did not, I just did not hang around that group. The problem was the way that the country was trying to keep kids at the time away from drugs was not honest.

"They made it sound as if you'd fall over dead or become a heroin addict if you took a single puff of pot or tried LSD even once. And we could see that was clearly not true. I think the other thing was the adults at that time made it a taboo." She laughed. "Anything that taboo was an open invitation to kids in my generation."

Cheryl went on. "But Frank, if they told my story, what happened to me during the next ten years, it would give a young person some pause before they took that first toke of marijuana. What happened to me is why I was so adamant about you staying away from all that stuff." Then she told Frank an honest story about her years in Portland, at times openly crying as she recounted her experience.

Frank had to force himself to not react seeing how difficult it was for his mother to tell Frank the things she was telling him now. Frank kept quiet, displaying little emotion.

She told Frank that the relationship with her high school boyfriend lasted less than two months after they moved to Portland. By the end of the summer of '68, Cheryl and her high school boyfriend went separate ways, leaving Cheryl to deal with life on her own. Like the lyrics of Bob Dylan's song "Like a Rolling Stone," Cheryl's own life rolled down a path leading to her lifestyle becoming a classic example of the worst of the '60's lifestyle. "*To be on your own... With no direction home...*"

Maybe the law in physics that says as mass gains momentum in any direction, it tends to maintain that momentum and direction, is also accurate for life in general. Over the next seven years, Cheryl's life continued, and accelerated in the same manner on an ever-accelerating downward track.

"Maybe dumping my old boyfriend was the first mistake I made. But we were really just friends. I wasn't really in love with him or anything," she said with a smile. "He was and still is a good person whom I still consider a good friend."

She said with a broad smile, "You know, Frank, your mom was a pretty young girl at that time and could turn more than a few heads... pretty sexy!"

Frank tried to ignore such a comment from the person he knew as his mother, just asked, "So who was he, Mom?"

"He's someone who still lives here, Frank. I do not think it's a good idea, nor is it important to tell you his name. We split up when I fell for this other guy. I met him the first few days in Portland. Turns out this was not to be anything good either. He was drafted before the end of the summer."

He was drafted into the United States Army. Just a month or so after she met him, he was in basic training. By December, he was en route to Viet Nam, arriving in Saigon in the middle of that month. A month or two after his arrival he died violently in downtown Saigon at the start of what became known as the 1968 Tet Offensive.

Cheryl was on the edge of sounding hysterical. "That was the problem with that stupid war. If you were less than a middleclass boy, you had a good chance of being drafted, and within a few months you'd be fighting a war halfway around the world that no one could explain why we were fighting!"

Cheryl had tears in her eyes as she told Frank how her lover had died so abruptly.

Frank said, "Mom, I want to hear this, but I don't like seeing you cry like this."

Cheryl pulled her emotions together and then calmly said, "It's okay, Frank. I need to tell you all of this so you can see where I was when I met your dad." She half smiled at her son. "It gets worse.

"I was pretty distraught when I got the news just a few days before Christmas. What was strange is that I was numb with grief, but I kept partying like nothing had happened.

"I have to tell you that I was a mess. I would get off work, and stop and get a bottle of wine, the cheap peach and strawberry flavored stuff that everyone was drinking then. I'd smoke a joint by myself when I got in, and then sit in front of this little black-and-white TV until about nine or ten.

"I'd go back out to the store and get another bottle of wine. Smoke some more pot and then drink about half the bottle of wine before I went to sleep. I'd finish off the rest in the morning before I went to work."

Cheryl explained that it was not long before she was not working at all and found herself living in a small rundown abandoned house, in a very rundown part of Portland, living with anywhere between seven and 13 other people depending upon the specific day of the year.

With a smirk on her face, she looked at Frank and said, "We had the nerve to call this place a commune. If we were living in that kind of place now, we'd call it a Crack House."

No one paid rent, but there was also no electricity, or gas, water or telephone service. They kept their communal household warm in the winter by gathering wood in the forest just outside of Portland and burning it in an old wood stove that was already in the house when occupied by this group of squatters. A garden hose ran from a neighbor's house, who apparently felt it was better to get along with this group, so as a result, they did have access to water to cook and occasionally clean themselves.

"The commune was not really a bad thing at the time," Cheryl said to her son Frank. "When it all started, everyone looked out for each other. It surprised many people that we were able to take care of ourselves so well. There was always food, and that old wood stove kept the house toasty during the winters. And there was definitely a strong sense of common ideological purpose. We were all united behind protesting the war.

"It's also interesting that I really cut down on the drug and alcohol use, at least at first. But it's also where I was introduced to real narcotics. But that came later.

"A few of us had jobs. I got another job as a waitress, about the only thing I could do. Others contributed by working to take care of the housing needs. We all put the money into a common pot that everyone used. There was one girl who had two children who lived with us, that we all assisted parenting.

"Initially, we wanted to change the world... end the war. It was what happened to me personally that kept my life spiraling downward. The really bad stuff started again at the end of the year," Cheryl explained.

In December of 1969, Cheryl took a motorcycle trip with a man who had taken up residence in the commune a few months earlier. She ended up with a group of bikers in Oakland, California. The reason for this trip was to attend a rock concert in the hills to the east of the San Francisco Bay area. If she knew that she was hooking up with the infamous Hells Angels, she might have made a different decision.

The week she spent in Oakland was worse than any time she had been out on her own thus far. She and her biker friend stayed at a "crash pad" with four or five other men, and several very tough women. Cheryl said this group was very dirty, aggressive, and always high on speed.

She had sex with every one of them, men and women both, in ways she would have never imagined in her most horrible nightmares. She could either do what she had to do to survive or run the risk of losing her life by defying these drug-crazed people. Cheryl chose survival.

Cheryl said, "This was not something I wanted to do, but I really thought if I did not, something bad was going to soon happen. So, I did."

Cheryl told Frank that the next weekend, Saturday, December 6, 1969, she and this biker rode the twenty or so miles to the hills in the Altamont Pass for the concert that later became known as Woodstock West.

At first, it was somewhat enjoyable to Cheryl, although it was on the rowdy side with several fights erupting throughout the event so far. She had decided that as soon as she could, she was going to break away from the man who brought her, lose herself in the crowd, and figure out a way to get back to Portland on her own.

Although for the moment, she allowed herself to enjoy the music as much as possible. Earlier, she saw her favorite rock group, Crosby, Stills, Nash and Young, perform, although it too was interrupted by a fight.

The Rolling Stones had started their performance when her "friend" dragged her up next to the stage alongside a couple of other bikers, other Hells Angels members, who apparently, depending on who's telling the story, had something to do with concert security.

While the Stones were performing "Under My Thumb," Cheryl heard what sounded like a loud gunshot and turned to see a young Black man being stabbed multiple times by one of the bikers. Cheryl saw the man dying, a couple of feet from where she stood.

"I can't tell you, Frank, if that man was shot, stabbed or both. What I can say is this man was doing nothing but watching the concert from what I could tell, and these Hells Angels, so called security shot and killed him for no apparent reason."

Cheryl continued to explain that as the crowd broke up, she managed to separate herself from the biker with whom she had arrived at the concert. She literally begged people to give her a ride anywhere to escape. Cheryl caught a ride to Sacramento with a group in a crowded Volkswagen van. A couple of days later, she hitched up Interstate 5 to Portland, and back to the commune.

"So Frank, do you understand now why I get so pushed out of shape when I see you associating with the same kind of racist bigot that I have personally seen take a life over hate? I see your friend Ben going down this same path and get worried that you are going to get sucked in with him," she said.

Frank started to answer, "Mom, I am not...." But Cheryl shook her head, saying, "I'm sorry. I'm getting off track. Let me finish this story, Frank," said Cheryl.

Cheryl explained that for the next several years, she continued to live in the commune until the city forced the actual property owners to evict the squatters and later destroyed the old structure.

"After the commune came down, I was really on my own. I am not going to tell you about every living situation I was in over the next seven or eight years. But I'll say that I saw a lot of the bad parts of Portland and some of the worst people in this world.

"I will tell you that I ended up falling back into that group of bikers off and on. I could never completely shake that group as long as I was living in Portland," she told Frank.

She explained to Frank that it was this group that sucked her deeper into the hardcore drug culture, and even into prostitution. However, in her present living and economic situation at the time, she could no more escape this group of bikers, any more than she could shake the blue out of her eyes. The word trapped was an understatement in describing her situation. Somehow, she managed to survive for nearly five more years in her little section of Hell.

Cheryl said, "My friend Sally saved my life, Frank. I think I'd be dead if it were not for her."

Frank asked, "What happened to Sally?"

"I honestly don't know. I lost track of her when I moved back to Mama's and had you." She smiled. "I guess you took precedence after that. But she was much smarter than me, so I am sure she is doing fine, wherever she is."

She continued, "About a year after I met Sally, I literally opened my eyes one morning and decided this life was over. I concluded it was time to get out of that lifestyle, or certainly die."

In 1976, Cheryl had befriended Sally, who started talking to her one day while Cheryl was "*spare changing*" in Portland's downtown area.

Sally Jones appeared to be about the same age as Cheryl and worked at a daycare center from which she would bring the kids to the park along the river in downtown Portland, where she would see Cheryl, but had never spoken. One day Sally walked up and started talking with Cheryl for some unknown reason. Perhaps Sally merely decided it was time to find out why Cheryl appeared so troubled.

The two of them would sit and talk several times a week. This turned into a ritual that went on for about a year. Then, one day, in an act that is nearly unheard of, Sally invited Cheryl, a near total stranger, to live in her apartment until she could get herself on her feet again. Cheryl decided when she opened her eyes the following morning to accept Sally's offer.

Unlike Cheryl, Sally was far more conservative, and far removed from the drug and alternative cultures around Portland. Taking the whole situation as a gift from God, Cheryl stopped using any drugs cold turkey. She had a lot of motivation. She thought if she went out soliciting drugs that group of bikers would again find her, returning her back into that old lifestyle that she had come to despise.

Seeing the earnest change in Cheryl, Sally helped her get a decent job at the daycare center where Sally worked. It seems that the mass had lost its momentum in the down direction and was finally trying to establish motion going upward.

About two years had passed when one day Sally told Cheryl, with whom she had established a very good friendship, that something had developed, and she had pretty much decided to move to Sacramento, California, at the end of the month. Specifically, Sally told her that she had a distant cousin who lived in Sacramento, who had just purchased a motel, restaurant, and bar from their aunt, following the death of their uncle the previous year.

As she explained it, this was really a great situation. She was going to be able to live for a while rent free in a small apartment complex adjacent to the motel that the family owned, in exchange for working at the motel. Of course, they were going to pay her too.

Sally figured after a year, she could claim being a California resident, and start attending one of the community colleges in the area that were still inexpensive for California residents.

"I don't think Sally realized that she was not going to have to twist my arm very much to get me to tag along," Cheryl said with a little laugh.

Frank said, "I don't understand. Why didn't you just get up and move back to Grandma's a long time ago?"

She answered him. "I don't know, Frank. I think people become caught up with where they are. At that age, I wanted to do it all on my own terms, I guess. When I was in the middle of it all, it really did not seem that abnormal. It was just my life, and I adapted to it. I was amazed when I realized how fast nearly ten years of my life had passed. It seemed like one big blur.

"The thing was that when I met Sally, I could see that I wanted to change my life. We may be who we are, but every day you wake up, you can change your life."

Cheryl continued, "So Sally told me that this apartment was large, big enough for both me and her daughter to share. Like I said, it really did not take a great deal of pleading to convince me to tag along with her to Sacramento. I certainly did not have a better plan, so I immediately agreed."

The fact was that Cheryl did not want any part of the past to find her. She was trying to put distance between her and her past, and this was going to put six or seven hundred miles or so between her previous lives.

"So, in effect, Frank, I just dropped out of Portland without telling anyone anything. Matter of fact, I did not tell Mama I had moved to California until I had been there for nearly three months. As far as I was concerned, I just wanted to get as far away as possible, and I hoped no one from my life in Portland would ever find me.

"For that reason, once in Sacramento, I started going by my middle name, *Margaret*. It was about two years later that I met Fred, or should I say, that Margaret met Fred." She laughed. "It was Margaret who struck up the conversation with Fred at the Dew Drop Diner."

# CHAPTER 5

## Fred and Cheryl

"You can see how I might be ready for something good to come into my life, I think. I had settled into Sacramento for several years and had put Portland and everything about that lifestyle behind me. I liked living there."

Frank asked, "What about the men from those bike gangs?"

"No, Frank. I never saw any of them after I left Portland. Just to be safe, I kept using my middle name Margaret as long as I lived there. But I still had a tinge of fear when it came to men in general," she explained.

"I can see how you'd feel that way after what you went through," Frank interjected.

Cheryl continued telling Frank how she and his father had met in the restaurant at the Dew Drop Motel. "I can still hear that danged country song that was playing on the radio the day I started talking to Fred. He had been coming into the restaurant every morning for a week or two. But on that morning, I started a conversation with him," she told Frank.

"That's why you always turn the radio up whenever that country song comes on the radio," Frank mused aloud.

"Yeah, I guess it is... never really thought about that, Frank," Cheryl replied with a laugh. "I remember the first words I said to Fred were 'You seem to like that sad country song, cowboy,'" as she continued telling the story of meeting Fred for the first time.

"I reached over for the coffee pot and asked Fred, 'Would you like some more coffee?'"

Fred's face lit up and a broad smile instantly appeared, replacing the somber look he was showing a moment earlier.

Fred replied, "Well, yes, I think I will have some more coffee. Yes, I do like that sad country song... reminds me of someone." As Cheryl poured the coffee, Fred continued, "So if I like a country song, does that make me a cowboy?"

Cheryl laughed and said, "No, but that brand-new-looking Stetson hat and shiny lizard cowboy boots I always see you wearing is a dead giveaway. And yes, if I see a man that can sit and listen to those songs without going crazy, I will say that he must be a cowboy. Those songs are just too sad—cheating wives, getting drunk, getting into fights... way too sad for me."

She giggled again. "And the song that was just playing, that you were so into is really too sad... a woman drowning in a river?"

"Naw, Merle Haggard made up that song after his dog drowned. Fell into the river down in Bakersfield and got swept off and drowned. Really... that's a fact. It was on the radio a week or so ago. You know, I met Merle Haggard at a grocery store in Redding once... really nice man," said Fred.

"Well, he must have really loved that dog," she said with a laugh. Cheryl added, "Now me... I like rock and roll... and soul music."

"Oh. So, are you a hippie or a Negro?" Fred, like some White Americans, still used the word "Negro" when referring to African-Americans, even in 1982. Even the term "hippy" was long out of style for at least the last ten years, but not to Fred.

Again, Cheryl laughed, and sarcastically asked, "Do I look like I'm Black?" She moved forward and leaned over close to him, and then placed her forearm next to his, just barely touching his arm, but making her interest in him a bit obvious. "See, I am as White as you."

Fred laughed and said, "We're both free, white, and legal age."

Cheryl went on. "But I do like a lot of soul music, like Kool and the Gang and Michael Jackson. So, cowboy, what is your name?" She stepped back and then added, "By the way, most people don't use the word Negro anymore. I believe they like to be called African-Americans unless you want someone to think you're a bit of a racist."

"Fred is the name; Freddy is what my friends call me. And Freddy prefers Negro, and he is not a racist. Don't know what that means no how."

For some reason, this made Cheryl start laughing hysterically. She said, "Freddy... you really are a cowboy!"

"Yes, I am," replied Fred without missing a beat. "And I even worked on the Hearst Castle Ranch breaking horses," as Fred started to recount one of many stories he would tell "Margaret" about his life's experiences. Fred had no problem talking about his adventures and loved to tell a good story. If the subject were one that Fred wanted to talk about you could not shut him up. On the other hand, you could not pry vulnerable information out of him with a crowbar.

Fred sat and drank far too much coffee while talking with "Margaret" until the late morning when the Saturday lunch crowd started arriving. Blame it on the coffee, the more he drank, the more and faster he talked. Their conversation that morning revolved mostly around irrelevant small-talk subjects, but enough for both to internally conclude that they seemed to like each other.

Although Fred was fifteen or so years older than Cheryl, Fred looked to be only a few years older if not about the same age. He had a 1950s appearance, a combination of Elvis Presley and James Dean would fit the description of his look and style. At 35, Cheryl was a beautiful woman. Fairly tall at five feet, eight inches, very slim in an athletic way, blue eyes, brown hair in a practical short hairstyle, youthful in her presentation, with an air of a woman who has seen a lot of the world, and is okay with her place in it.

Fred complimented her with his tall, handsome appearance and youthful smile. It really would appear they were made for each other. Thus, it should come as no surprise that as Cheryl walked out of the restaurant at the end of her shift that afternoon, Fred was sitting on the big shiny chrome bumper of the 1956 black Cadillac limousine that he had restored inside and out and kept in immaculate condition.

As she walked up to him, Fred with a long innocent smile on his face simply asked, "You wanna go for a ride?"

"A ride," Cheryl asked, "a ride to where?"

He smiled and said, "I have a friend who asked me to take care of a couple of horses whenever I am working nearby. I've been driving out there a few times a week after I get the rig put away. Thought you might want to go up into the hills where it is a little cooler for a few minutes. If you aren't afraid of a horse, you might even be able to help me a bit."

A ride up in the hills did sound good. It was a typical hundred-plus-degree summer day in the Sacramento Valley. Besides, she was very curious about this throwback to the fifties cowboy-like man with whom she had spent the morning talking.

"Okay. Are we going in that?" Referring to the thirty-year-old shiny black Cadillac behind him.

"Oh, yeah. We can't take that big truck. That Cadillac goes everywhere I go. I rebuilt the engine and transmission myself two summers ago... runs perfectly. I've taken it to Alaska and North Carolina. I even drove her down to Mexico a couple of summers back..."

Fred was about to go on nonstop talking about the car until Cheryl broke into laughter and stopped him.

"I believe you, Freddy! Just let me change into something more appropriate for being outdoors."

About an hour or so later, they were in the coastal hills, about fifty or so miles northwest of Sacramento, driving on a winding country back road between the Sacramento River Delta and Clearlake.

You would think that someone who drives a truck for eight hours a day would hate driving if one did not have to. Not Fred. Fred could get off work on a Friday after spending the entire day driving a truck and on a whim, get into his '56 Caddy and the next evening, find himself in a country/western bar in Flagstaff, Arizona, having a beer and swapping stories with men he worked with in the past. Then he would be back in his rig in California come Monday morning for a full day of work.

Everyone seemed to know Fred, wherever Fred and Cheryl stopped. When they stopped at a gas station in Williams along Interstate 5, as they were leaving, the owner of the station ran out to give Fred a referral to wax a local farmer's airplane at the little crop-duster airport.

Even way off the main road at a roadside market in the town of Guinda, a very rural town if you could call it that, in the hills along Highway 16 where he stopped to get a couple of soda pops and some chips, the clerk called Fred by his first name like he had known him for years.

All the time while driving, Fred told stories, and "Margaret" laughed, almost ceaselessly. Finally, a little after five, and after opening and closing half a dozen gates or so, along dirt roads running far back into the hills, they drove up to a corral out in the middle of nowhere. There sat an old truck trailer that had a big rusty dent along the trailer's front roof that looked as if it had hit the bottom of a highway overpass.

Stacked alongside the trailer were about twenty or thirty bales of hay covered with a black tarp. Inside the adjacent corral, seven young horses walked up along the corral fence with the appearance of a Norman Rockwell painting. They seemed to know that something good was coming with the arrival of the Caddy.

"This is a quaint little spot, Fred."

"It most certainly is. You know, Margaret, this is not really a job to me. I love driving up here," Fred musingly replied as he parked next to the trailer and shut off the engine.

"Let's get them something to eat," Fred said as he put on some gloves. He stepped out of the car, walked over to the old trailer door, and dialed numbers into the heavy-duty combination lock. Then he stood up on a bale of hay and pulled the door up.

Cheryl followed and walked over next to him. It was indeed cooler, partly because it was the latter part of a July afternoon, but also because they were a couple of thousand feet up in the coastal foothills with a bit of an ocean breeze coming through the passes. It felt good.

"Margaret, could you toss about a quarter of one of those bales over into that corral?" He reached into an old crate.

"Here… put on these gloves so you don't prick yourself," he said as he held out a pair of old oversized leather work gloves. She took the gloves from his hand and started pulling them on.

"Break them up into seven pieces and spread them apart, so they'll all get fed. That big guy is a little greedy and will try to eat it all himself." He picked up one of two well-worn saddles and started carrying it over toward one of the horses.

Cheryl asked as she followed Fred, "Who owns this land and all these horses, Freddy?"

"Fella named Ben Roundhouse, a full-blooded Indian," said Fred as he started putting the saddle onto the animal.

He continued, "Lives about three or four miles down that dirt road where we saw the mailboxes, the first right turn after the gate where we first came in off the main highway. He has me trying to get these little creatures to be a little less skittish. So, you'd be helping me if you would ride this one here for a while." Cheryl was throwing hay into the corral.

Fred stopped putting on the saddle for moment and asked, "You do ride?"

For some reason, this made Cheryl start laughing, and she said, "Yes, Freddy, I can ride."

As Fred saddled the two horses, it became apparent to Cheryl that Fred had something special when it came to dealing with these animals. The fact is that Fred had quite a reputation when it came to training horses. He had been working with ranch horses for most of his adolescent and adult life, and it showed when he was around them.

"Come over here for a moment, Margaret," Fred said. "Let me show you a little trick. You'll have them eating out of your hands in no time."

Cheryl approached Fred somewhat apprehensively, not knowing what to expect, she said, "Okay, Freddy, show me this trick."

Fred had already pulled out a burlap bag filled with honey oats from the trailer. He instructed, "Put a handful or two of these oats into each of your back pockets.

"Now Margaret, step through the fence and get into the corral with them. Don't be afraid," Fred continued. "You have to let them know that you are the boss and you're not afraid of them."

All seven of the young horses walked up and were all trying to sniff Cheryl's back pockets.

"That's the way, Margaret, perfect. Now, reach into your back pocket and get a bite-sized amount in your hand and put your hand directly under the mouth of one these ponies you want to reward. Make sure you keep your hand flat and the tips of your fingers curled back as far as you can, so he doesn't accidentally bite you."

"Oh, Freddy, this is so neat," exclaimed Cheryl as the bigger of the horses slurped the oats off her hand.

"Now Margaret, every so often give a different horse a reward, just so they don't get jealous. Think of them as young kids," said Fred. "Don't give it all to them at one time."

Fred laughed. "After you come up here a few times with some oats in your back pocket, they won't be able to wait for you to do whatever you want with them. They'll be following you around sniffing at your butt all day long, oats or no oats."

Cheryl broke out laughing. "Just like the men at the restaurant do!"

For the next couple of hours, they rode back into the hills on that July evening. Cheryl would tell you that this date, if that is what you would call it, was about the most romantic event that had ever occurred in her life so far. Moreover, that was good, because for the last few years, Cheryl was about as skittish with men as these horses were. Cheryl would also say she was in love with Freddy by the time he dropped her off at her apartment, adjacent to the Dew Drop Motel late that night.

For the next four or five weeks, Fred and Cheryl saw each other nearly every day. If he spent the night in Sacramento, he was in the restaurant at five in the morning when Cheryl was opening the restaurant. If he were on the road the night before, he would see her as soon as he got the rig put away and cleaned up.

They would go for rides into the gold country in the Sierra Nevada Mountains, go to the movies, or just go out and have dinner together. On Sunday, when they were both off work, they would spend the day at the Roundhouse ranch in Guinda, where Cheryl would watch Fred work with the horses, and maybe later take a ride back into the hills. She was fascinated with the rapport and skill he had with these animals.

What they were not doing was sleeping together, not that Cheryl would have had any problem whatsoever, starting on day one of their relationship. Cheryl was looking forward to sharing that level of intimacy with Fred. She also thought it would probably be a lot of fun for them both.

While Cheryl was a product of the 1960s hippie generation, Fred being much older and coming from a God-fearing southern family was much more conservative when it came to things like sexuality, intimacy, and gender roles. In fact, Cheryl and Fred did not share their first kiss until about two weeks after their first date. Fred had also fallen in love with Margaret.

Ironically, both Fred and Cheryl were independently plotting on just how and when this elevation in intimacy would take place. Fred's world was very compartmentalized, and although Fred was far from being any sort of virgin, women fell into two groups, the kind you play with, and the kind you marry.

Without any doubt, in Fred's mind, Cheryl was part of the latter group. Fred would tell you that in his life, he had come to "know" a number of "painted ladies" in reference to the first group of prostitutes and women of less-than-high reputation. Fred's life experiences were that of a cowboy, complete with saloon girls and farmers' daughters.

In Fred's assessment of Margaret, she was a farmer's daughter. He obviously knew nothing of Cheryl's previous life. He never asked.

By the end of August, the Sacramento Valley agriculture related truck-hauling work that kept Fred employed during this time each year was beginning to wind down. Fred would soon be going back to his permanent home in Fresno, where he would spend the next month mostly hauling San Joaquin Valley grapes and raisins to processing plants in the Fresno area. Cheryl knew this and started planning the big event for the coming Saturday night.

The big event in Fred's conservative mind between he and Margaret revolved around if he wanted to marry Margaret. He was playing with just how the whole process would work.

Cheryl had sized things up from the beginning and started planning this evening after their first date. Sally and Cheryl attended a lingerie party a few weeks earlier, and Cheryl found just the right attire for the big event. For Cheryl, it was all about intimacy, although she was not opposed to the possibility of setting up housekeeping with Fred.

That Saturday evening was indeed very romantic. Cheryl had prepared an excellent dinner in her apartment, including cold champagne, soft music, and lots of candles. She thought it was a perfect evening with a perfect man. To seal the perfection of the evening and their new bond, shortly after dinner, they did make love.

Later, Fred did ask Margaret to join him in Fresno. However, Fred felt compelled to tell Cheryl about himself, his family, and some of the not-so-pretty things he went through. He told her about running away from home when he was ten and riding the boxcars out west. He told her how he ended up in a chain gang in Texas, just because he was camped along the railroad tracks without any money. He told her about how he injured his knee while in the Army.

He told her many things, some that were very shocking to her. Such as when a man who physically threw him off a moving train, nearly killing him. He told Margaret of another incident when he was beaten up and left out in the wilderness for dead. The circumstances of these incidents were so shocking that Cheryl had a major change in her feelings toward Fred. She gave no answer to Fred's invitation to join him in Fresno.

The next morning, Cheryl begged off going to the ranch in Guinda. After Fred left, she packed everything she owned into her 1978 Toyota Corolla,, and drove to Bend, Oregon. She left instructions with Sally not to give Fred any information about her. That was the last time she ever saw Fred, and she never again saw Sacramento after that day.

Fred was devastated when he got the news that Cheryl had left. The next morning, he returned his rig to his employer, telling him he had a sick relative and had to return to his home in Fresno that morning.

Five weeks after Cheryl had returned to living with her mother in Bend, she discovered she was pregnant with Frank. She told her mother that she had no idea who the father was, and knowing of her lifestyle in Portland, her mother took that as the truth.

That is the story she told her son Frank, although the version she told Frank was highly edited to keep it a "PG"- or at the most "R"-rated narrative.

As Cheryl concluded telling Frank her story, she looked at Frank, saying, "You see, Frank, as far as Fred knew, my name was Margaret Malloy, and Margaret rejected him in a bad way. I don't think he ever tried to find me... he had no reason to. Mama and I agreed we'd raise you on our own."

Frank said to his mom, "I did not know that you went through all that. I had no idea of what happened to you in Portland, Mom."

His mother was weeping openly when she said, "I never wanted to tell you about the horrible mistakes I have made in my life. My life has some real ugliness that I never wanted to face. And they are all about my decisions, including the decision I made about your father."

She continued, "I did not find out that I was pregnant with you until after I had been back in Bend for several weeks. I tried to find Fred to tell him, but I could never locate him. I swear to you, Frank, I tried."

"Nothing about what I have done should ever be placed onto your shoulders. This has nothing to do with your life, or who you are," she added.

Frank thought about all his mom had told him and came to understand why his mom had always been so evasive about talking about her past, especially her relationship with her father. He leaned over and kissed his mother.

"Mom, I love you," he said.

"Thank you, Franklin, you have no idea how much I love you."

55

Over the next four years that Frank was in college, and the years after when he was in his twenties, Frank never gave a second thought about his father beyond that he would have liked to have known him. He did feel his mom had indeed been frank and earnest with him.

Little did Frank know that his mom had still left out some key details that he would not come to know for many more years.

# PART II

## The Tedders

*"... One child grows up to be, someone who just loves to learn.*
*Another child grows up to be someone you'd just love to burn.*

*Mom loves the both of them, you see it's in the blood... Blood is*
*thicker than mud, it's a family affair..."*

*Sly and the Family Stone - 1969*

# CHAPTER 6

## Franklin's Journey

Frank hated traveling to Fresno for a couple of reasons. For one, the airline connections were about as bad as they could get. If he had a morning appointment in town, he had to fly in the day before and spend the night. Moreover, in Frank's view, the weather was always atrocious. It seemed that it was either unbearably hot or socked in with the worse fog he had seen anywhere in the country.

Hot to a person from Portland, Oregon, was anything warmer than the mid-eighties. Frank knew you could almost count on it being at least that warm in Fresno, starting in late April and running through October. Even worse, during the summer months, Fresno is always well over a hundred, nearly every day.

However, Frank was pleasantly surprised when he arrived around noon on Sunday, November 2, 2008. It was neither foggy, nor overly warm, actually in the mid-60s with a few clouds, a perfect day as far as he was concerned. The locals on the other hand seemed to act as if it was freezing!

He walked down to the end of the terminal building to pick up his rental car. Smaller airports had at least one consolation in that you did not have to walk from east to west *Hell and back* to get from one place to another. He got his rental car and started the drive to his motel, about twenty minutes or so on the northwest end of Fresno, and about five minutes away from the following day's worksite.

As Frank drove, he thought about how much he loved his job. He was 26 years old and already a manager, in charge of client services for Pluto Software, a small software company based in Portland. Frank had been working, or at least hanging around Pluto for as long as nearly any of the full-time staff.

He became involved with Pluto during his freshman year at Oregon State University in Corvallis, Oregon, while taking an elective class in general computer technology.

His instructor was a gray-haired man who came to class dressed in plaid double-knit pants, and a button-up sweater worn over a golf shirt, that would have been stylish if he was the former President Gerald Ford out on the golf course in 1976. However, Frank found that this instructor was brilliant when it came down to explaining how computers functioned at the most basic level.

When he covered the introduction to the computer programming subject area, Frank was fascinated because of the graphic examples this instructor used. He could imagine the computer system as a series of pipes with a fluid flowing through them, and by controlling how different valves changed the flow, and how that could change the flow of a different set of pipes, it could control what was stored and/or output into different containers.

Although this may not have made much sense to everyone else in his class, in Frank's visual mind, it made things perfectly clear, and it was just a matter of knowing the names and properties of the structures and learning how to create the logic to control the data flow.

When he did his programming project, he turned in a program that made his laptop act as a very advanced clock radio, much more than anyone had even attempted. What was even more impressive is that he controlled the clock's accuracy by plugging into U.S. Government's official clocks over this new thing called the Internet when many lay people thought that it was a new expansion of the Federal Highway system.

His instructor was intrigued with the extra effort and encouraged Frank to think about changing his major to computer science. He also gave Frank a recommendation for a summer job at Pluto Software, a small tech company that was just established about a year earlier in Portland, about eighty miles from the OSU campus.

Frank made minimum wages, plus a couple of McDonald's coupons thrown in for essentially being a gopher... *go for* this or *go* to the store *for* that. But he enjoyed it. It beat flipping McDonald's burgers. He especially liked hanging around Pluto Software's two full-time programmers, asking them questions about how to do certain things that he would go home and try on his own computer.

As the summer of his first year's employment at Pluto was ending, along with the end of his summer job, Frank, really by accident ended up solving a tough programming problem that was delaying the release of one of Pluto's school administrative program versions. Public school districts represented Pluto's largest client base.

The specific procedure had to do with creating a data model that extended results in such a way that made some statistical predictions when a given school district's attendance condition changed. The goal was to provide the school district with a way to pre-empt attendance problems before they happened.

A few weeks earlier one of the programmers explained to Frank about how they were approaching the problem. Frank thought their idea was a cool concept and saw a use for something he wanted to try. He started working on an application that he could use to predict his own performance in his schoolwork, and a few days later brought his code in to show the two programmers. His solution was a little crude, but it worked.

Twenty minutes after he showed one of the programmers what he had built for his own program, he found himself sitting in a conference room with both of Pluto's full-time programmers, as well as David Brewer, the owner of the company, explaining to the group how the logic of his solution worked. In fairness to the Pluto programmers, Frank came up with his solution precisely because he was not a seasoned programmer, living by all the rules.

At the end of the meeting, the owner, a then forty-something African-American transplant from San Diego offered Frank a part-time job during the regular school year, along with a fifty-cent-an-hour increase in pay.

The job was perfect, because for the most part, Frank could work from his apartment for 12 hours during the school week and drive into Portland for eight hours in the office every Saturday.

Although he was working from his home, he worked under the supervision of the two full-time programmers. They also stipulated that Frank could never spend more than his set weekly hours on work, just to make sure he did not start neglecting his college education objectives. David Brewer also threw in a pizza coupon with each paycheck, and for the rest of his school employment provided him, to his initial surprise, with a $250.00 check at the beginning of each term to help with his books.

Mostly, Frank tested programs to make sure that they worked properly before new software installations or updates went out to their clients' systems. However, on Saturday's when he was in the office, he did a little of everything, including writing computer code, working the customer support telephones, and even selling products and services. The people at Pluto, including David Brewer were extremely pleased with Frank, and the company provided him each year with a raise in pay.

Frank graduated with a Bachelor of Science degree in Computer Technology and immediately went to work full-time for Pluto Software as a programmer, overseeing the coding done by the off-site part-time programming staff. He was completely in charge of product testing. He was salaried at $60,000 per year, not too bad for a young man just out of college at the turn of the millennium in a city the size of Portland. Of course, David Brewer made sure they threw in an extra pizza coupon with each check, a practice that continued the entire time he worked at Pluto. It was hard to break a tradition.

Frank had both the right temperament and skill set to be the top-notch programmer he was becoming. Additionally, Frank had a highly creative mind, in addition to possessing great people skills. Everyone liked Frank, both his coworkers and the clients, and he contributed something to just about every area of the small company.

Thus, two years later, Frank became the primary person who went out to the client sites to install and integrate the Pluto products into their clients' existing data systems, as well as providing onsite customizations for Pluto's school district customers in the western United States. This meant that Frank was on the road at least three out of four weeks a month, and occasionally had assignments that would keep him at a site for up to two months.

Anyone who has been a *road warrior*, traveling every week knows that you come to either love it, or hate it. As an energetic single young man that wanted to experience everything the world had to offer, Frank was part of the love it set. He always tried to plan his trips so he could see something the place had to offer if it were not anything other than driving to a scenic geographic site and taking a few pictures. In addition, he was racking up airline miles that he used on vacations to indulge in his favorite pastime activity of scuba diving in cool places around the world.

So far, this trip to Fresno had not been so bad, thought Frank as he pulled into the motel parking lot. The airport security screening in Portland was quick and uneventful, his flight both departed and arrived on time, his rental car was ready without any snags, and the weather was decent. What more could a road warrior, such as he, ask?

Frank checked into the motel. After dropping his bags in his room, he headed down to the bar to have lunch and catch part of whatever football game was still on. Frank was not much of a drinker, but a couple of beers did sound good while watching some football. Heck, he thought, he would have probably been doing the same thing if he were still home in Portland.

Turns out, he had come to the right place at the right time. He came into the restaurant bar just after the start of the second half of a San Francisco 49er game. San Francisco was leading by a touchdown. Apparently, this was a 49er hangout, and everyone was happy and very lively.

Frank sat down on one of four barstools surrounding one of the small round tables adjacent to the main bar. When the waitress came by, he ordered a beer, and asked for a menu. A few minutes later, the server returned, and he ordered a burger and fries for lunch, being careful to ask her to have the cook not use any butter on the hamburger bun and absolutely no cheese. Frank was extremely lactose intolerant, both as a child, and even more so as an adult. As he waited for his meal and sipped on his beer, he got into the game like everyone else in the room.

It was while Frank was staring up at the television that he felt someone bump against the back of his chair in the crowded bar. He turned around and the man standing behind him just said, "Excuse me."

"Oh...," Frank said as he looked up from the hamburger he was eating and saw a somewhat short and kind of round man, at least twice Frank's age. "Don't worry about it. It's a crowded room. Great game, though."

"Yeah, you're right," said the man in a way that sounded like he couldn't care less. He moved around to the opposite side of the table, so he was directly in front of Frank.

"Actually, he continued, I think I know someone who is related to you," the man added with a mid-eastern accent.

"Huh? You must have the wrong person. I don't live here, I am just passing through on business this week," Frank replied.

"No, no, trust me, I am fairly certain. My name is John Assorian, and when I saw you come in, I went out to my truck and got this thing I've been carrying in my glove box for the last couple months." He let out a slight laugh and added, "Need to clean out the truck sometimes, I guess. Here, look at this if you would, sir?"

Frank was in the middle of chewing on a bite of hamburger when John handed him what looked like a church program or something.

However, when he focused on the document, what he saw made Frank quickly swallow a half-chewed bite of food so he could reply, "Where did you get that picture of...," and he stopped, realizing it was someone else.

He was looking at a funeral or memorial service program that had a picture of a man who looked almost identical to Frank. Change the clothes and add a more modern hairstyle, and he would have been looking at a picture of himself.

However, it was what he read that made him pause. It read "Fred L. Burton, Jr." The "*L. Burton*" part was meaningless to Frank, but the first name was enough to make Frank quizzically ask, "Did you know this man?"

"Oh, yes, I knew him very well." John was from Armenia and although he had lived in the United States since he was a child, he still spoke with the slight accent of his first language. He spoke low, and amid all the noise in the room, Frank had to listen very carefully to understand him with the still lingering accent.

"I knew him as well as you would know anyone that you've seen and talked with at least a few times a week for fifteen or twenty years. He used to come into my restaurant nearly every day during the week, sit at the same place at the counter for breakfast and talk to me, or anyone else who accidentally sat next to him." He laughed.

His face changed to a sadder look, and then John added, "I miss him these days. He passed about two months ago," he said while pointing at the program. "You know, I used to own this restaurant. Started it from nothing," making a gesture with his hand.

John stopped himself from digressing into elucidation of his thoughts about the restaurant and went on. "It's hard to forget Fred. He came in several times a week from damn near when I opened... and we spent so much time talking.

"I hired him to detail the cars I owned over the years. I've had him into my home. Fred was honest and loyal... he was an incredibly good man. Yes, I would call him a good friend."

The last couple of things that John said compelled Frank to ask, cautiously, the next two questions. "Did he ever live in Sacramento?"

Frank had to lean forward to hear John's reply. "Not that I can recall in the time I knew him. But I think Fred was a bit of a drifter in his early years. He lived a very different life, and I think he lived in a number of places around the country," John replied.

"Was he a truck driver by chance?"

"Come to think of it, he did drive trucks," answered John. "Why, do you..."

"Sir, my name is Frank Malloy," Frank sounding excited, cutting off John's reply. "If you would not mind, I'd like to talk with you some more over in a quieter section, without all the noise in here."

"Sure," replied John, perplexed by the sudden increase in interest. "Let me get the waitress." John motioned to the server, who quickly came over to the table.

"Hi, Big John," said the very pretty waitress. "What do you need?"

"Selena, could you move us over to one of the tables in section two?" John pointed to a table in a room that was separated from the bar area with an open partition.

"Sure. It's not open, but you may pick any table and I'll take care of you."

"Thanks, dear," John replied. "Come along, Mr. Malloy."

Speaking to Frank, the waitress asked Frank if he was finished with his lunch to which Frank replied he was, and he and John got up and moved out of the bar into the restaurant section. Once settled, John picked up the conversation.

"So, you think this man may have been related to you then... no, Frank?" John then asked, "Should I call you Frank?"

"Of course, you can call me Frank. I am still thinking about what you have just shown me, John, and I am very puzzled. I really don't think anything, except that this *could* possibly be a relative of mine on my father's side," Frank carefully replied.

"The fact is, I know little about my father and his family. I never met him, and my mother has never told me a great deal about him," Frank added.

"I have always hoped I would find out who he was. I feel strange when I think this man who fits some of what I know is now dead. No way this could be my father."

"Oh," replied John. "You think he might be your father?"

"Yes, the thought did cross my mind. It is possible from what you just told me along with that picture," replied Frank.

John said, "I really understand about not knowing your father. I came over to this country when I was a little boy to live with my uncle and aunt. I was maybe five years old. You see, Frank, both my parents were killed in the violence of war. I would even be dead, no doubt, if it were not for my uncle and aunt. I don't even remember what my mother and father looked like. There is only one old picture of my father when he was a boy. No pictures of my mother... nothing. Only the stories that my uncle tells me about his brother and my mother are left."

"No...," Frank said sounding a little irritated. "You don't understand. My mother has nearly refused to tell me anything beyond the most basic information about my father..."

"Young man," John interrupted the beginning of what was sure to be an anger-tinged tirade, "you are going to have to start learning how to accept information without anger, and just be satisfied with that. Otherwise, you are going to spend your entire life being angry with everyone who tells you something you don't like."

"But...," Frank started to reply and again was interrupted by John.

"No, no, no... no buts," said John. "I tell you what. I met some of Fred's family at his funeral last month." Reaching for his wallet in his back pocket, John went on. "I think I have his niece's phone number with me."

He pulled out a fat wallet stuffed with papers and cards. John shuffled through some cards and slips of paper and pulled out one folded note and said, "Yes, I do."

"Are you going to call her right now?" Frank asked.

"Sure. Why not," replied John. "If you would let me use your phone." John did not have a cellphone himself like just about everyone else in America. He thought it was just a gimmick to get more of your money.

Frank took the sheet of paper, picked up his phone and entered the phone number, and then passed it back to John. "Here you go," Frank said, and handed John the phone that was now ringing, loud enough that Frank could hear it ringing across the table.

Frank heard a tinny-sounding woman's voice answer, "Hello?"

John spoke into the cellphone, "Hello. Is this Gayle?"

"Yes."

"Gayle, this is John Assorian," replied John. "*Big John*, I met you at your uncle's funeral."

"Oh… I remember you. You're the man with the restaurants," Gayle said upon recognizing to whom she was speaking.

"Yes… well, I used to own the restaurants. Not anymore, I'm afraid."

Gayle asked, "How have you been, John? I wanted to thank you for saying such nice things about my Uncle Fred. My mother and my brothers all appreciated what you said about Uncle Fred."

"That was not hard, Gayle. Your uncle was an incredibly good man, and he was entertaining," John added with a laugh. "Didn't you see how everyone just loved to hear his stories?" asked John.

"Are you kidding? He'd drive us all nuts telling them over and over again." Gayle laughed and said, "We will miss hearing them, won't we?"

"I already do, Gayle," said John and changed his tone. "Gayle, I was wondering if you were not too busy right now, if you could come over to where I am and have lunch. If not today, maybe we could meet later this evening or tomorrow?"

Gayle, a little perplexed, asked, "Oh… is there anything wrong?"

"Oh, no. Nothing like that. I was just sitting here telling someone that knows of your uncle some of his stories and like, and I thought you might be able to share some of that with him." John added, "He was not able to make the funeral, you know, and he is just visiting from Portland for a day or two this week."

"Maybe," she replied. "I was just about to go out shopping, John. Where are you now?"

When John said he was at his old restaurant, just a few minutes away, Gayle agreed to drop by within the next half-hour before she went out on grocery shopping chores.

It turned out to be a little less than twenty minutes when John saw her working her way through the crowded bar toward the unopened section of the restaurant where Frank and John were seated. Upon seeing Gayle, John jumped up and quickly walked over to her, took her hand, and said, "Hello, Gayle," and then hugged her.

There was only one problem with this picture, Frank saw an older, attractive, and very well-dressed African-American woman. This did not make any sense to Frank. A flood of thoughts went through his mind in a matter of a few seconds.

# CHAPTER 7

## *Frank and Gayle*

Frank sat perfectly still, without much of an expression on his face. In his brain, he was trying to make some sense of what was transpiring. Now, the woman who John was leading back toward their table was obviously a Black woman that John said was Fred's niece. Following this logic, if this woman is Fred's niece, Fred could not be his father. Right? After all, he knew he was white, and no one in his immediate family had ever even hinted otherwise.

Frank decided to keep his mouth shut until she offered more information. Maybe this family has multiple marriage relationships, and this Fred is not really a blood relative, Frank thought.

Although... as he thought about this a little deeper, a shudder went through his body. His mother had always been very cagy about talking about his dad. He could see how this information might be something his mother would think she would want to "protect" him for his own good. Nonsense... even with that intent, you would think she would have told him something to prepare him for an event such as what was quite possibly taking place.

As John and this woman approached the table, the objective part of Frank's brain kicked in, and he decided to hear a bit more before coming to any conclusions and thus passing judgment on anyone. He put on a look that he hoped did not betray any of the emotions that had rolled through his mind in the previous seconds.

"How nice it is to see you," John continued as he guided her over to the table and pulled out a chair for her.

"Thank you, John," Gayle replied. She was obviously a little rushed, and at the same time, she could not keep herself from glancing at Frank seated to her left. It was also apparent, that she was trying not to stare at Frank, but she kept glancing at him with a look that said, "*I should know who he is.*"

John said, "I want to introduce you to Frank Malloy. This young man is here in Fresno on business this week."

She turned and looked at Frank a little quizzically and said, "Well, it is nice to meet you, Frank."

"I am also happy to make your acquaintance, Gayle," said Frank.

At that moment, it finally struck Gayle about what was unusual about Frank, she said, "You know, Frank, you look just like my uncle. You even sound a little like him."

"So, you think so too," Frank immediately said back to Gayle. Frank had a very strange look on his face, as he added, "Seems like that is the consensus around here these days."

Seeing Frank's look, along with his somewhat condescending-sounding reply, Gayle replied to Frank, "I can see that you are happy to meet me," and she started to get up when John patted the top of her arm, motioning her to sit down.

"Gayle…," John in a subdued voice said, "… the two of you need to talk. I know this is very strange, but I thought, unless we, how do you say, put all the cards on the table, the two of you might not ever get a chance to meet and talk. I think it is important that young Frank talks with you. Now Gayle, please have some lunch, on me." John called to the server on the other side of the room, "Selena. "

"I have already had lunch," Gayle bluntly said.

"Well, have some pie then," said John with a large smile. "They still make them here using my old recipe. It's rather good," he added with a smile and handed her a menu.

"Understand that young Frank is not all together comfortable with what he is discovering this Sunday afternoon." John continued. "He walked in here thinking he was going to have a quiet off day watching football and drinking beer. It looks like your 49ers won, by the way."

John kept going, saying, "But I interrupted his afternoon with that picture." He pointed at the funeral program. "And now he is considering things that he had not given even a thought a few hours earlier. So, Gayle, please sit and have some pie for a few minutes before you go off shopping."

Gayle, a diabetic, thought about the chance to have a forbidden piece of pie without her husband here to stop her, and instantly agreed. John motioned Selena over and ordered some peach pie for Gayle.

John then turned and looked at Frank. "Young man, you are going to have to learn how not to be so threatened by information that you don't necessarily agree or want to hear. By the way, Gayle, I've been meaning to ask you. " He turned to Gayle and asked, "Do you have a relative named Louis Meyers who once owned a scrap metal and junk business, maybe in the 1950s?"

"Yep, that was my grandfather."

Turning back to Frank, "That's what I mean, Frank. I thought I recognized the name and asked my uncle after Fred's funeral. My uncle did business with Gayle's grandfather.

"He would buy parts for an old car they used to drag race out in Raisin City back in the fifties when he was a teenager. Her grandfather had a successful business here in Fresno. I think that my uncle went to high school with Gayle's father, who became a local doctor as I seem to recall my uncle telling me. He knew Gayle's father quite well. You see, Frank... you should only hope you are connected to this good family."

Gayle said, "The truth is that Uncle Fred did mislead us. It wasn't until he was on his deathbed that we found out that he had two lives, one as our uncle, a Black man, and another with a group of people who thought he was White that apparently included you, John." She chuckled. "He kept this stuff separated for his entire life, right here in the same town."

Frank interjected, "Well, I never knew your uncle. My mother only told me about a man named Fred Langton is my father, but she never ever hinted he was Black. This man has a different last name." However, Frank was thinking his mother had told him she had lied about Fred's last name. He did not mention that fact to John and Gayle as he made the last statement.

Frank went on talking. "I don't think we're talking about the same man." But the look on Frank's face betrayed the negative thoughts that were going through his mind, causing John to lecture a bit in a driving delivery.

John looked directly at Frank with a very stern look. "You want to talk prejudice and hate? I know all about prejudice and hate. I am here with just my uncle because of prejudice and hate. My mother and father died in the old country over prejudice and hate. I would do anything to know more than just my uncle. I would not care who they are."

"But this man was not very proud of his family. He must have lied to everyone, even his own family," Frank said with some distain. "Besides, I never said I thought he was my father."

John leaned back and sighed. "You know nothing about this man, Frank. I knew him as a very decent man. The truth is that I was very puzzled when I went to his funeral and saw all the Black faces. I had no idea why they were there until the service began and they introduced them as his family. You see, I had not talked to anyone. I went when I saw the funeral announcement in the newspaper."

John let out a little laugh. "I could see about half the people at the graveside were White, really looking like… what do they call them… let's say country white people so I don't use one of the bad-sounding words: jeans, cowboy hats, and cowboy boots." He laughed some more.

"It was very funny. I could see that many of the Whites at the funeral were glancing around looking as surprised as I was. The funny thing I thought at the time is it would have made no difference if Fred were Black or White. I think anyone that sits in your business nearly every day and is as talkative as Fred would have got to know me. And I would have liked Fred by any way I got to know him."

But his expression changed to a thoughtful look. "You know, I have to admit that as open-minded as I like to believe I am, I cannot honestly say that I would have taken the time to get to know Fred if he had more African appearances and features. That would surely have been my loss. But I guess I too can make decisions based on first impressions of what we have been taught to be good or bad. How much we have lost," as he trailed off into thoughts regarding his own family.

"Well," as he picked back up in a strong tone, "young Frank wants to know more about this man, my friend and your uncle, Gayle." He laughed a bit and added, "He just does not yet know he wants to know!"

"Just because he looks like Uncle Fred, does not mean that he is Fred's son," Gayle stated between bites of her surprisingly good peach pie.

Frank not missing a beat added, "You got that part right!"

"And to finish my thought, Frank," said John, ignoring Frank's last comment continued. "If you were living with the Nazis during World War II, and a Gestapo man walked up to you with a gun pointed at your head and asked, 'Are you a Jew?'"

John turned his head and stared right at Frank and asked, "How would you reply, Frank?"

"Hell no," Frank answered firmly.

"Of course, you would. And sometimes people just trying to survive get caught up in what they felt they had to do or say… to survive."

"I can see that," Frank said, and then in a very analytical way added, "But I don't see any reason, any real evidence to support the idea that this man Fred has anything to do with me beyond coincidence. Please don't take offense to this, Gayle.

"But being very blunt, I sincerely hope that it does not turn out to be true. He lied to everyone, he was uneducated, and spent his life drifting from place to place, job to job. He was a truck driver and car cleaner. I can go on without this man being part of my life," Frank finished.

Gayle looked at John, who smiled and shook his head, as if saying, "*Okay, I tried.*" Then, Gayle, sounding a little angry, said, "You know, Frank, my uncle may not have fit into your high standards, but I for one think he was an outstanding uncle.

"My grandmother came to Fresno from North Carolina after my grandfather died. My mom asked her to move out here where she knew no one, so she could help her take care of us when we were little kids. I think my mother wanted to help Grandma get through the loss of her husband right after he died in the early fifties. I was maybe five years old."

Gayle started calming down and went on. "But that's when my Uncle Fred started showing up. The truth is that my mom and my uncle did not seem to be close at all. They would argue about stuff that really did not make any sense to me. My dad never got into these arguments, which I thought was a little strange, because my dad had an opinion about nearly everything.

"I do remember thinking that my grandmother and Uncle Fred looked very alike. Uncle Fred even then always was dressed as a cowboy that I as a little kid thought was cool. But what I remember most was how close he was to my grandmother. He always appeared to me to be a big kid when he was around Grandma.

"He'd come by and pick up my grandmother in one of those old cars he owned. My brothers and I would all climb in with them. He would take us to the mountains, to the beach, and a lot of times, just driving around in the country. He would tell my grandmother and us kids stories about the different things he had done, or the places he'd seen. The fact is he did a lot of different things and had travelled to a lot of places in his life.

"He had this way about making what he said rhyme when he was telling a story, or just cracking a joke." This last statement made Frank perk up and pay more attention. "For some reason, I always remember him saying, 'Have you heard the joke about the rope?' Then he'd say, 'Just skip it.'" Gayle laughed.

Frank with a little smile just said, "Really?"

"Oh, yeah, Frank, he could make you laugh, even when you did not want to," said Gayle. "I remember my brother Eric when we were little kids, was playing with an electrical cord. He was chewing on it with the cord plugged into the wall. My Uncle Fred walked in catching Eric, looked at him, and just calmly said, 'Boy, you better stop playing with that cord before you shock your britches down.' It was so funny the way he said it in such a straight matter-of-fact voice."

"He could be so calm in an emergency. One evening, during the summer I think, my uncle took my grandmother and I out for a ride, and we saw this unbelievably bad accident occur, right in front of our eyes. It was so weird, as I got older, I would have to ask my uncle from time to time if it actually happened.

"The sun was just going down, when about a quarter of a mile ahead, a car going extremely fast went through the stop sign, colliding with a car going down the highway. One car launched into the air, almost straight up, and tumbled over at least once, before landing in a cloud of dust. What was so weird, and what made it seem so surreal is we did not hear a sound.

"My uncle sped up and then as he approached the accident turned and parked the car in such a way that I could not see the accident without getting up, turning around, and looking through the back window. My grandmother was in hysterics, and Uncle Fred told her not to let me look at the accident, and then grabbed a flashlight and went out to help the victims.

"It was horrible, even though I could not see; I can still remember a woman who screamed for a long time before she went silent. There was a fire, and apparently, Uncle Fred pulled two of the victims out of the overturned car before it burned. He later told us that the screaming woman was trapped beneath the car. He could not pull her out, and she died in the fire. I remember he was crying on the way home."

"You know, Gayle," John interjected, "Fred told me the same story, although he did not talk much about what he did, or how he felt. I had no idea that he saved two of the victims."

"Well, Uncle Fred was always long on story, but very short when it came to things that weighed on him emotionally." She turned to Frank. "I don't think he would have even responded if you asked him why he would lie about his heritage. In fact, he would tell us that he never saw any racial discrimination when he was riding the boxcars in the thirties and forties, that all of us had a little trouble believing."

"He would say that he saw some horrible things, and had some horrible things happen to him. I always just thought he was in denial. I understand a bit more since he died."

Frank added, "Or, maybe he did not see any discrimination because there wasn't any."

"Or maybe," said Gayle, "… he meant he never experienced any discrimination as long as people thought he was White. And that answers the question why he was not exactly upfront and honest in that regard, doesn't it, Frank?"

"Fred definitely preferred to tell stories that were entertaining," she continued, "like being picked up by Rock Hudson while hitching from LA."

Frank, looking a little puzzled, asked, "Who is Rock Hudson?"

Both Gayle and John looked at each other and started laughing, and Gayle asked, "Who is Vin Diesel?"

They all started laughing, even though Frank was not exactly sure why.

Gayle looked at Frank and said, "Frank, I've decided it really is good to meet you, but I have some things I must get done." She turned to John and thanked him for treating her to a piece of pie.

Then she thought a moment before she added, "Frank, I am going to leave you my phone number, and I want you to call me if you have questions, or just want to talk. Maybe I could take you over by my mother's house before you go home?"

"Thank you, Gayle. But I don't think that will really be necessary," replied Frank.

Writing down the phone number, she said, "Well, make me happy and take the phone number anyway, in case you change your mind. I really do hope you work this all out."

She handed him the slip of paper, said goodbye to John, and left.

After Gayle was out of earshot, John looked at Frank. "I misjudged you a little, it appears. Nevertheless, I have a feeling you are going to end up using that phone number. Maybe it's not a bad idea to meet and talk to Gayle's mother before you leave?"

Frank was laughing as he replied to John, "Are you kidding? That is some of the most ridiculous crap I have ever heard. I'm really a Black man? Please. That's absolutely crazy. No. I don't need to know any more."

John also laughed when he started his reply, "Do you have a girlfriend, Frank?"

Frank's first thought was to tell him that it was none of business, but instead answered, "Yes, I do." He would play along for the moment.

"Is this serious? I mean, are you thinking about ever marrying this girl, or maybe someone else, ever?" asked John.

"Maybe, but this is none..."

John held up a finger and said, "It is your business. Because I wonder how much you will be laughing when you explain how your son or daughter that you just brought home looks like it is a little Black baby?"

"Yes, Frank," said John, nodding his head, "It has happened, more than you realize."

"And these days, Frank, even if something that dramatic does not happen... these days with DNA tests being used all the time to screen for possible health issues, how long do you think it will be before your son or daughter comes to you to ask why you did not tell them they were Black?"

Frank was silent as John went on.

"You see what I mean? This is not something you will be able to avoid you see, not these days. But you are in a place where you can find out for sure about who you are, and maybe know something about the rest of your family. Wouldn't you rather know so you can have an answer? I guess the real question is, can you stand not knowing?

"I suggest you might want to talk with Gayle some more, and maybe her mother. And if you think that Fred might be your father, you can have one of those DNA tests. You think about that, young Frank."

Frank started to reply, "I think I will...," but was cut off by John.

"Now, young Frank, I need to get home before my wife thinks I have finally left her." John motioned to Selena and got the check. Then he reached into his wallet and plucked out a single card.

"Frank, it was good to meet you and I wish you good luck. Call me at the number on the card. I'm afraid I have never got into this whole cell telephone thing. Don't want my wife to find me so fast."

"Thank you," said Frank. "I will think about what you said. Believe it or not, I am glad we met and had this talk. By the way, who is Rock Hudson?"

That made John laugh and he just said, "Kids. Good luck, Frank."

John got up and walked out of the restaurant, leaving Frank sitting to reflect on the afternoon. After a few minutes, he too got up and walked down to his room and turned the television on.

The news was on, and all news was about the Presidential election. Somehow, what had been something just analytically interesting to Frank, took on a new meaning. It really looked like the country was going to elect a Black president. Frank did not cast his vote on his absentee ballot for Barack Obama a few weeks earlier.

As he lay on the bed, he thought about his arguments for voting for Obama's opponent, the Arizona Senator John McCain. Frank's argument centered on the generalized idea concerning higher taxes, and proliferation of a new healthcare program, that to him sounded ridiculous considering the present economic crisis that had emerged some months earlier.

However, as he thought about his feelings, the real reason why he voted in the manner he did was because he was a little nervous about Obama. Like many people, Frank thought the name itself seemed to be a little un-American. The name "Barack Obama" sounded to him as a person likely be subjected to search prior to boarding any airline. In fact, he was convinced if Obama were not a Presidential candidate, he probably would be on a watchlist in these times, just because of his name.

Moreover, even though Frank had read most of Obama's book, and had a particularly good idea of his education and background, he had this little thought that Obama's educational achievements had more to do with affirmative action. The reason why he had that underlying thought was that like some others, Frank tended to group Black people with college degrees with affirmative suspicion.

Now, Frank thought, the mere suggestion that God, with a devious sneer may have given his genetic kettle a quick stir was throwing off the way he rationalized his most basic decisions. To top it all off, he had no idea how this was all going to come out. The question that rolled around in Frank's mind was John's parting question: "…can you stand not knowing?"

Frank's cellphone rang with the distinctive ringtone of his girlfriend. He said aloud, "Thank you, Barb, for pulling me out of these messed-up thoughts," and then on the next ring, he pushed the button on the phone and said, "Hello, Barbie Doll."

"Frank, you know I can't stand for you to call me that," the woman replied.

Frank laughed. "You didn't seem to mind that a few nights ago."

"Well," purred Barbara, "in that situation, you can call me anything you want." She went back to her regular voice and continued, "But Frank, we did not decide what we were going to do about the dinner party my boss wants us to attend Friday. You said you were going to go more than a month ago."

For the next fifteen minutes, Frank and Barbara talked, mainly about the dinner party Friday evening. Although he had only known Barbara for a few months, he had to admit, the question John had asked him earlier that day was truly relevant because he did have serious thoughts about Barbara. Barbara and Frank worked out the details about their attendance at Friday's dinner, and then Frank said something that from Barbara's view came from out of nowhere.

Frank asked, "So, Barbie Doll, how would you feel about going to the dinner with a Black man?"

"Huh?" Surprised by the question, Barbara was not sure where Frank was going as she gathered her thoughts and replied with a laugh. "The last I knew, I was going to the party with you, Frank. Did you finally learn how to dance, and turn into a Black man in the last twenty-four hours?"

But Frank was not laughing when he said, "Of course not." Then he paused, got his thoughts together, and then let out a short-subdued laugh and added, "Obviously I am not Black, honey. I was talking with a guy in the bar earlier and thinking about something he was saying very hypothetically. I am a bit curious if you would go out with a Black man."

Barbara thoughtfully replied, "Frank, I've gone out with Black men in the past. So, if you are asking if I would go out on a date with a Black man, sure I would. I hope you are not setting me up for someone else to take me to Dr. Salinger's dinner this Friday."

"No. You know I wouldn't do that." Frank continued, "I just said that I am going to be there, and I don't see any problems with Friday. This is just generalized discussion. I am not trying to test you or anything, Barb. I was simply curious about something that made me think about how people interact in general. Let me pose the question in another way. In general, if you were not dating me, would you seriously date a Black man? You know, maybe think of getting married, maybe having children someday."

"Well, if it was a Black man like David," Barbara was referring to David Brewer, who introduced her and Frank, "I would have to give it a great deal of thought. But in general, Frank, I'd have to say no. There are so many different things that are involved with marriage, even between two people of the same race and share the same values.

"My father would be one big consideration, and the other major concern would be what the children would have to deal with in life. Although, if I loved someone like I love you, that would complicate things regardless of what color, or for that matter, anything else they were.

"I don't think any woman would willingly set her children up from birth to have a hard road for their entire lives." She kept going, saying, "You know, Frank, I dated a man in college that was Black, and my father and I went about two years before we could just sit down in a room without a major fight after that.

"And the funny thing is that my father is not a racist or anything like that, at least that is what I thought at the time, and still think now. Times may have changed a little, but there is still a lot of backwards thinking in that regard. Now tell me, what's this all about, Frank?" she asked.

"It's just what I said, Barb. It was about a nothing conversation at the bar earlier. Actually, I said almost exactly what you just told me." The last part that Frank stated was not true at all. Frank shifted the conversation. "Will you still be able to pick me up from the airport on Thursday?"

The conversation went on for a few more minutes, mainly about their arrangements for the end of the week, and then they hung up. Immediately, Frank knew that he had no choice but to get closure to the chance encounter he had earlier with Gayle and John. He reached into his pocket and retrieved the now crumpled note with Gayle's scribbled phone number, and then clicked the text message button on his phone. He typed the following message:

*"Frank from rest today. Would like to meet your mom B4 Thur PM. Pls call this num tomorrow. Frank M."*

Frank thought a moment, and then pressed the "send" button. Three or four minutes later his cellphone buzzed with the following short reply: *"OK. Let me know when and where. Gayle."*

And that was that, thought Frank. He thought he was going in a direction that he really did not want, but he felt he had little choice. He realized he could not stand not knowing the facts. He got up off the bed, took a shower, and went to bed. His last thought as he drifted off to sleep was that he did not have a choice as to who his father and his family were. He was going to learn a great deal about Fred Burton and his family over the next few days.

# CHAPTER 8

## *Riding the Boxcars*

*"... I say to you that today, even this night, before the roos-
ter crows twice, you will deny me three times."*

*Jesus speaking to Peter*

-Holy Bible, Mark 30

*"... I do not know this man of whom you speak (said Peter)
... a second time the rooster crowed... and when he thought
about it, he wept."*

- Holy Bible, Mark 71-72

It was late, very dark, and very cold, but Fred was happy to be gone from what
had been a nightmarish experience. He felt like one of the runaway slaves that
his mother had told him about in stories. Fred was walking along what barely
qualified as a country dirt road, amid the rocks and chaparral brush in North-
eastern Nevada, about eight or so miles from a major road. It was just after
midnight, and he thought if he kept up the same pace, he would reach the
main road by dawn, where he should be able to hitch a ride out of this section
of Hell.

He was not afraid of being out alone this night. This was not the first time
Fred had found himself on a long walk at night in the middle of nowhere. He
was very hungry and afraid... afraid of capture. The trick, Fred thought, was
to let your mind wander and think of anything except walking, and just let one

foot keep ahead of the other. Fred let his mind drift and thought about the day he left his birthplace of Durham, North Carolina, many years ago.

He remembered the day he left home as if it had just happened last week. It was late September, and the weather was changing from summer into autumn; a few nights before, it had been very warm and humid. Now it was much cooler with a cold crispy feel to the air. Not cold but much cooler than it had been just a few nights before… it was fall. However, it was cold enough for him to question the wisdom of the plan he was going to execute in the morning.

What had forced his decision in his nine-year-old brain was what had happened the day before. Instead of walking to school the previous morning, Fred had taken a detour, and took a walk out into the woods on the edge of town, where he and his sister Mattie had found a spring earlier in the summer.

Since then, this had become Fred's special place. He was fascinated with the way the water came out from beneath a rock alongside a hill, and from nothing flowed and continuously filled a creek. For some reason, it always made him think about traveling to all the places he had seen in movie newsreels with his sisters.

Before he knew it, it was afternoon, and he knew he needed to get home to keep his mother from becoming worried and worse, start investigating and find he had never got to school. Unfortunately, Julia, his mother, was waiting at the door when Fred walked up that afternoon.

"Fred," asked Julia in a very angry voice, "why weren't you at school today?"

Fred did not reply. He just looked up at her with tears wailing up in his eyes. Although tall, Fred had not yet eclipsed his mother in height.

Hearing no reply, Julia said, this time as a command, "Tell me where you were, Fred!"

"I was down yonder at the spring Mattie showed me," was his reply, in an obvious attempt to bring his sister into it.

"No, Fred, your sister came home with Mrs. Peters from the school. She walked her home to talk to me." Julia continued, "Mrs. Peters says you missed another day last week, where did you go that day?"

Openly crying, Fred could only calm himself enough to say, "Yes, Mama."

Fred's mother was very perplexed about Fred's attitude toward school. He was extremely smart. Things like reading and math came quite easy for Fred, and yet Fred absolutely hated going to school. His sisters on the other hand loved going to school, and they fully comprehended what education meant.

However, Fred was nine, and the idea of the rest of his life had not yet become a reality to Fred. Fred's mother also remembered that this value was not automatic with Fred's three sisters, especially Mattie. If the situation was not so bad, she might have laughed when she remembered how Mattie on her first day at school came home the same morning, and she had to convince her to return.

Fred was not Mattie, and Julia's other concern was keeping her husband, Fred Senior, from beating little Fred within an inch of his young life. Fred's father would have zero tolerance when it came to threatening his son's education.

So, Julia looked at Fred and said, "Fred, go outside and get me three switches off the tree."

Fred started uncontrollably crying. "But Mama. I was just down…"

Julia said, "Just nothin', Fred Junior. You bet' not say another word! You better get to gettin' them switches, now, Fred Junior!"

As Fred stomped out, Julia was thinking that she was really trying to spare Fred an even worse whipping by his father. She thought if maybe, she could sting his legs a little with the switches, Fred's father would see the minor welts on his legs, and hopefully, think the punishment she provided was enough.

Fred remembered it was not enough. His father came home early that evening and was furious, giving Fred one of the worst whippings of his short life so far. The nine-year-old Fred had no clue in his young mind why his father would physically punish him so severely.

Like many children that are the focus of their father's punishment, Fred had begun to think that his father hated him. This emotion would seal into Fred's psyche, even until today, as he walked through the high Nevada desert.

Walking along the road, Fred upon hearing rustlings in the bushes just a few feet in front of him to his right was jolted back into reality. Fred's heart started to beat extremely fast, until he recognized the deer for what it was. The animal, without missing a step, stealthily bounded over the barbed-wire fence on the opposite side of the road in a single effortless jump and quietly disappeared into the darkness.

Fred stopped for a few minutes, surveying up from where he had come. He figured it was well after midnight, and he had been walking a good four or five hours, so he was maybe close to halfway to the main road that came down from Idaho and hooked up to the highway that headed west to California in Elko.

Not seeing any headlights, or any other signs of anyone looking for him, he continued his walk, and again let his mind drift back to the day he left home.

After Fred's father had delivered this last whipping, Fred Jr. had enough, and decided he was going to leave home that very night. Fred had heard men talk about riding the boxcars and thought he would just go down to Durham's railyard that ran along Fayetteville Street and get into a boxcar and wait for it to leave.

Thus, after everyone in the Burton house were fast asleep, Fred slipped out and retrieved the burlap sack where he had earlier stashed a few belongings and walked downtown to the railroad yard.

To the nine-year-old Fred, his plan was to just to find a boxcar that had an open door, get in, and wait for the train to leave. The only problem was that there were armed guards all over the railyard. Fred only found locked boxcars on sidings outside the railroad yard as he poked around. Finally, Fred found one car unlocked and open, connected to a string of other cars along a siding track, outside the yard.

He climbed in where he saw it was about half filled with empty 55-gallon oil barrels, stacked three high. He selected a place behind some of the barrels and cowered down in the corner with his burlap sack and waited for the train to leave.

The excited Fred sat in the corner of that boxcar until the sun came up, and then all day... it never moved. As the sun went down, Fred just sat in the corner. He was beginning to think that he needed to work out a few flaws in his plan. However, he was well past the point of no return. He cringed at the thought of returning home and imagined getting something worse than a whipping.

However, sometime while alone in the dark boxcar, the sounds of someone else climbing into the car interrupted his lonely musings. He froze. His first thought was that it was one of the railroad guards. He heard the person moving around like he was settling in, setting things onto the floor of the car. A few moments later, a flickering light that Fred recognized to be from a candle gave some dim illumination to the train car's interior.

The young Fred shifted and tried to cower back further into the corner and bumped one of the barrels.

Immediately, the man said with thick southern drawl, "Who dat?" The man got up and cautiously walked back to where he heard the noise emanate. As he walked back toward the corner, he held the candle out to illuminate Fred, trying to be as small as possible. What the man saw when the light illuminated Fred was obviously a boy, probably in his mid-teens judging by his size.

What Fred saw was the face of a man with horrible-looking tobacco-stained teeth, two or three months of beard growth, and filthy clothes. The man smelled as if he had just crawled out from the bowels of an outhouse.

Looking at Fred, the man ordered, "Git da hell out hea, boy."

When Fred did not move, the man barked a command. "Come out hea, boy." Then in a tone that sounded like he was forcing himself to sound friendly, the man added, "I ain't gonna hurt 'cha."

When Fred crawled out and stood up, the man saw that he was a big kid, about five feet five inches tall. He figured he had to be about 14 years old or so.

"You waitin' on a train, boy?" He let out a little scary-sounding laugh.

Fred replied, "Yes, sir… I was hopin'."

The man started laughing in a scary way and said, "Well, you be hopin' wrong, boy. This train ain't goin' nowheres. Not you and dis train, boy."

The man laughed again, a little more normally, and added, "You see, boy, jes 'cause they be a boxcar on a track, don't mean it be goin' nowheres. You wanna take a ride on a train?"

"Why, yes, sur I do. I wanna go to California like I saw at the movie," said the young Fred.

"California? How you gonna go to California if you can't even find a train goin' nowheres? You muss be runnin' from ya mama and daddy."

Fred spat back with anger, "My daddy beat me."

"Yeah… my daddy beat me too." For some reason, this made the man start talking a little friendlier. He went on, "But this ain't like catchin' no trains at the station. You gots to learn how. I'll show ya how tomorrow."

The man continued to speak to Fred. "The first thing you gots to learn is how to keep food in your belly. Come on out hea, boy, you hea?"

The man called himself Arizona Bill, apparently because he had made it as far as Arizona once upon a time in his pitiful life. Bill was a southern boy, through and through, and said he was from Mississippi. Arizona Bill talked a lot. He shared some of his food with Fred, a few sardines, some crackers, and part of a half-rotten apple. The next morning, he indeed showed Fred how to hop a boxcar.

As promised, Bill started instructing Fred the next morning. Outside the railyard, Arizona Bill started talking to Fred as if he were a schoolteacher. "Boy… the trick is to jump dat car when the train is jes startin' to move. Real nice and slow like. If you want to get inside, go down by the fence and find a boxcar that is open, and then wait for it to come out dat yard.

"Now you be reals careful when you is around that yard." Bill continued, "And don't let none of thems railroad dicks see ya." Bill was referring to the railroad detectives and guards.

"Them dicks don't take to us messin' with them rail cars no ways and will throw ya in jail or worse… maybe shoot ya. I seen dems shoot a niggah once. You ain't no niggah, is ya, boy?" He asked the question while looking at Fred with a somewhat serious expression on his dirty face.

Without missing a beat, Fred replied trying to sound indignant, "Why, no, sur, I ain't no niggah!"

"That be good. Arizona Bill don't take company with no niggahs! Maybe they jes tho you ina chain gang for a mont or two. You get fed ina chain gang tho, and that ain't so bad dees days, ya know, boy." Bill let out a short laugh.

Bill went on with his instruction. "When ya see dat train car come outta dat yard, you get to runnin' long side and you put boat yo hands on da floor of dat open door, an pulls yo'sef up in one jump. And you be's rea careful ya don't slip under dat train. Slice ya in haf' just like a hot knife goin' through cold grease. You got that, boy?" Bill asked, sounding extremely excited.

"Yes, sur," replied Fred.

"If'n that train be goin' too fast, you cans grab that brakeman's ladda at the end of the car and swing on, and den crawls under and ride stretched out in dat carriage under da car. But don't yous ever ride on top, or on a flatcar out in the open if'n you can hep it 'cause them dicks can see ya."

Just as Bill finished his last bit of instruction, a long whistle blew, and the big black steam engine in front of the train they were watching started belching clouds of thick white steam. The train slowly started to move forward.

Bill then said, "All rat, hea we go. You ready ta run, boy?"

"Uh-huh," came the reply from Fred.

Fred saw the big steam locomotive begin to move toward the position where he and Arizona Bill were couched at a slow yet increasing speed. Suddenly, Fred saw a man who was also hidden in the bushes began running out toward the approaching train, just a few feet in front of them. He sprinted down to the train, and jumped into a boxcar, just as Bill had described.

As the car that Bill had picked emerged from the yard, the train's speed was still slow, slow enough, Bill figured, for this boy to handle. Bill picked up Fred's burlap sack along with his own things rolled up in a blanket and tied with a piece of rope. He said to Fred, "Let's get to gettin'," and darted out, running along the car.

Once alongside the boxcar, Bill tossed the bags into the open door, and then put one arm into the car and expertly pulled himself into the boxcar in a single motion lasting no more than a second or two.

Fred, trying to remember Bill's instructions, did not have a clue in this real-world execution, and he quickly started to tire in his run, simultaneously trying to remember the instructions. Fred started to panic. However, Bill extended his arm, and Fred was able to grab hold. Bill pulled as Fred scrambled on, rolling across the stinky Bill. Once on board, his heart pounding, finally realizing he was safe and riding, Fred started laughing uncontrollably. He was traveling on the boxcars.

As Fred rolled off Bill and then rolled into a sitting position in front of the open door, he caught sight of about a half a dozen or so men, who would run out from along the tracks and disappear behind their car, looking like mice scampering to and fro.

As the train's speed was increasing to about the fastest anyone would be able to manage a boarding, a young-looking Black man ran out from along the tracks and tried in a last-ditch effort to climb onboard the car Fred and Bill were riding.

The man nearly slipped under the car, but he maintained his grip, got some balance and started to use his arms to boost himself up straight enough to try to roll into the open boxcar. Before the man could complete that maneuver, Bill walked over to him, and with his toothless grin full of hatred, he yelled, "Bill, don't ride in no car with no niggahs!" and then kicked the man square in the face, causing him to violently fall, and tumble along the tracks and then out of sight.

Well, that was enough to make Fred understand he did not want this man to find out that he too was what Bill would describe as a *niggah*. But Fred ended up tagging along with what he knew was God's poorest example of a human being for one reason, Bill knew how to survive, and Fred needed that knowledge if he too was going to do the same.

It is funny how symbiotic relationships develop. Although Bill was not in the front of the line when God was handing out brains, Bill was not exactly stupid either. Bill knew a good thing when it fell into his lap.

First, Arizona Bill had zero education. He could not read the single word on a stop sign, nor could he keep track of any number that exceeded the fingers on his hand. Fred, although he had only completed third grade, and had made no effort at his schoolwork, was a highly intelligent boy.

Just through taking up space in a seat at school, Fred had learned to be an above-average reader for his grade level, could write complete sentences, and even add and subtract. In comparison to Bill, Fred was a college scholar, and that had value, even to the repulsive Bill.

Second, when people saw Bill with Fred, they assumed that Bill was hauling around his son. That made Bill and his repulsive appearance look a little less threatening. Considering that Fred was a good-looking kid, people tended to want to help them. This meant that a farmer the pair might encounter was a little quicker to hire them for odd jobs, for pay or a meal.

However, maybe the biggest reason why Bill was motivated to keep Fred around was for shear safety. Two people, especially a good-sized kid such as Fred, helped, if nothing more than being an extra pair of eyes and ears. Bill and Fred rode the boxcars through the entire winter that year, getting as far south as Louisiana.

By the time they ended up in Kansas City, Missouri, in early spring, Fred had become an expert hopping the trains. He also knew many tricks to keep fed and stay warm. The two things that Fred never picked up was Bill's casual attitude for stealing, and his drinking habits. It was that last characteristic that led to Fred's final lesson from Bill.

It was somewhat warm in the late spring. Fred and Arizona Bill had hopped a freight car leaving a siding a few miles east of Kansas City earlier in the afternoon. Now at just after ten in the evening, they were well into Kansas heading southwest.

They had spent several days on a small farm a little east of Kansas City doing odd jobs for food, a shed to sleep, and a few cents of pay. The couple that owned the farm were childless and let Fred sleep inside their home. When they departed, the farmer's wife had given them a bag with some food, cornbread, some leftover chicken, and a few crackers and such.

Bill had also stolen a dust-covered, more-than-half-full jar of moonshine whiskey he had found a few days earlier while painting the kitchen. Bill had started *celebrating* just about as soon as they rolled aboard an open cattle car heading into the soon-to-be setting western sun. By this time in the evening, Bill was near intoxicated, actually about a quarter 'til drunk.

Fred sat near the door, watching the stars and an occasional glimpse of light go past in the darkness, while Bill sat on the opposite side of the partially open door. Bill leaning against the back of the wall was sputtering incomprehensible nonsense, with an occasional word he would say in a raised voice over the sound of the wind. He obviously intended for Fred to hear those heightened words.

Suddenly, Fred heard Bill say in a loud voice, "Get up, niggah!"

Fred had heard that same hate-filled voice before and was instantly in fear when Bill started to get up and stagger toward him.

"Thought I didn't know, didn't ya, boy?"

"I ain't no niggah," yelled a frightened Fred as he stood up and turned around to face Bill.

"Yes, you is. An' if'n you ain't, you should be. Kissin' up to dat white woman." Bill was referring to the farmer's wife who had taken a liking to Fred. "Don't no niggah boy like you have no bidness talkin' to no white woman. And Bill don't ride in no car wit no niggahs," yelled a hate-filled Bill.

He grabbed Fred by the collar, and yelled, "Get offa dis train, niggah," and violently pushed Fred backwards out of the door.

Falling through the darkness for what seemed like an especially long time, Fred had enough time to think to himself, *I am going to hit, and I am going to hit hard.* That is when he felt his back hit the ground extremely hard, then his head, and finally felt a sharp pain going through his skull like a nail driven by a hammer. Then it was mid-morning, with a man on a horse looking down at him. Fred was alive and in Oklahoma.

Fred stopped thinking about what happened to him 15 or so years ago and let his mind drift back to reality so he could assess his progress. He was still out in the middle of nowhere, still in Nevada, and still walking along the dirt road. Nevertheless, he was clearly making progress. Several more hours had passed, and he could see that there was a bit of brightness in the eastern sky.

He also could see an occasional headlight from a car or truck come and fade from view in a valley still some miles further. He figured the sun would be coming up in the next thirty or forty minutes, and he would probably make the highway in another couple of hours.

One foot in front of the other and let your mind drift, Fred mused. Fred thought how strange it is that we seem to do the same thing repeatedly. The truth was that Fred always had a twinge of guilt go through him, whenever he denied his family's heritage, especially his mother. To know Fred was to know that he loved his mother dearly.

Fred remembered how his mother used to tell him the Bible story about how Jesus told his faithful disciple Peter, who said he would never deny Jesus, that he, Peter, would deny him not once, but three times before the rooster crowed twice that very morning. Like Peter, Fred always felt guilty after he had told that whopper, and occasionally, he would slip up and tell someone the truth.

That had happened just two nights earlier when Fred was playing cards with his ranch hand friend Arnold. Fred found himself employed on this re-mote Nevada ranch as a direct result of his friend that knew of Fred's skill of working with horses. It was not as much as his skill with the animal, as it was an almost innate ability to get close to them in an almost psychic way. He loved the ponies.

Once hired on, Fred over the last year or so, had worked with about a dozen of this rancher's horses and developed them into well-trained working animals. Obviously, the rancher was impressed with Fred's well-trained cutting horses, and Fred being the personable man he was, spent a great deal of time with the rancher and his family. He and his friend, Arnold, received invitations into the rancher's home for dinner and such on a regular basis during the week.

Two nights earlier, Fred after a couple of beers, started talking a little too much, and told his friend about his family, including telling him that his family were negroes. To his friend, it was no big deal. He had known Fred for many years, going back to Oklahoma. However, the mistake was that his friend thought it was no big deal to everyone.

That evening, Fred, his friend, and the rancher were talking when his friend Arnold, just out of the blue, blurted out that Fred told him his family were Blacks. Arnold said it as a joke.

The rancher just laughed and said, "So Fred, you're a colored, huh?"

But Fred picked up a slight negative tone in the rancher's response. Fred, trying to figure out something to say, said, "Oh, no. My daddy was a white mailman, and my mother is a hundred-percent Cherokee Indian." The last part was somewhat true, his grandmother—his mother's mother—did have some Cherokee blood in her, but Fred knew she was indeed a very Black woman.

Fred went on to tell the rancher how his father would beat him, he said because he resented the idea that he was not his son. In the end, Fred could not tell if the rancher had bought the story or not. However, Fred could see that something had changed with the rancher.

But the next day, the rancher, as previously planned, drove Fred and a couple of other workers deep into the backcountry, at least five miles from the ranch, up into the higher desert mountains to look for cattle that strayed off while grazing.

Toward the end of the day, the rancher caught Fred alone tending to an injured steer. Unnoticed, he walked up on Fred from behind, and struck him hard on the side of his head with a large piece of wooden fencepost. He said, "You come into my home and lie to me and my family, you nigger? You aren't nothing but a lying nigger. I'm gonna kill you." He continued to strike Fred with the fence post. The only thing Fred could do was crawl up in a ball and try to protect his head as much as possible. The last thing Fred remembered before going unconscious was hearing the rancher say, "... if I catch you on my land, I'll kill you, nigger. You hear me?" and the world went black.

The next thing Fred remembered was waking up alone, out in the middle of nowhere at night. Fortunately, the rancher had not broken any bones, and with the exception of a severe headache, and a good-sized cut on the side of his head, he was without any life-threatening injury, and at least able to walk and think a bit in his post-dazed state.

It took Fred at least an hour or two to find his way back to where they had parked the trucks and the horse trailer earlier in the day. Now, twelve hours later, he was on the dirt road walking, but at least he was alive, albeit hungry, and very tired.

The sun had come up, and Fred could see he was about a mile or so from the main highway. About half an hour later, he was finally walking south along the main highway in the direction of Elko, Nevada. As cars and trucks approached, he put out his thumb in a gesture to hitch a ride.

After about fifteen minutes, a big rig with an empty flatbed trailer pulled over. Although hurt, hungry, and tired, Fred ran about a hundred or so feet to catch up to where the truck had come to a stop. He climbed up to the open window on the passenger's side and when he poked his head in, the driver cringed, taken aback by Fred's dirty and obviously beat-up appearance.

"What the hell happened to you?" the driver asked with a somewhat shocked expression.

"Some men beat me up and robbed me a few hours ago," replied Fred. "Can I catch a ride into the nearest town with you, sir?"

The man paused and assessed Fred and his situation, and decided Fred's demeanor seemed okay, and then said, "There ain't no nearest town out here, partner. I can get you to Elko, so climb in if that will do."

Fred said, "Thank you. That sure will do, sir."

The driver reached over and unlocked the door. Fred opened the door and climbed into the truck.

As they drove down the highway, Fred made up a story about how he was hitching the night before, and a car with three young men had stopped to pick him up, but instead, got out, beat him up, and took his belongings. Fred was an excellent storyteller, and the truck driver apparently believed him.

The truck driver asked, "Well, I guess you are going to want to go to the deputy sheriff's office when we get to Elko?"

"Naw. I saw those boys turn around and head back the opposite direction. They are probably somewhere up in Idaho by now," Fred replied. "They didn't take anything I can't easily replace. I think I am going to just try to make it on to California, where my mother and sister live."

"Well, you be in luck, partner. I am not heading all the way to California, but I can get you as far west as Reno. I'm picking up a load there and then headed back east to Salt Lake this evening," the driver said. "I'll tell you what, I'll stop at that truck stop on the west side of Elko, and let you get a shower and cleaned up a bit. Tend to them cuts and bruises. I got some time to make Reno. Maybe get something to eat. You got money?"

"Oh, yeah… I got enough to get something to eat. I always hide some money in my shoe, so them boys never found my money. Some food sounds mighty good. I have not had anything to eat since yesterday afternoon," Frank added.

The driver reached between the seats and pulled up a big bag of potato chips and handed them to Fred. He said, "You can snack on these until we get to Elko. You've got some money, so we'll get you some real food when we get into town."

In fact, Fred had every dollar he had earned over the last months he had been working for the rancher. He kept most of his money tightly folded and tied in a handkerchief that he kept safety pinned in his shorts, so the rancher did not find it while Fred was unconscious. He had transferred a few dollars to his pocket a few hours earlier for just this type of thing.

The driver went on. "I guess that makes as much sense as any. What's the point in reporting those boys now?" He laughed and said, "We're free white men, right?"

Fred replied in a lower voice, "We most certainly are." Then he added in a much stronger voice, "… free, white, and legal age."

Immediately, the driver stopped laughing when a passing car approached on his side of the road. The truck driver let out two long heavy-sounding blasts with the truck's loud horn, and the car darted back into its lane, narrowly missing hitting their truck.

For some reason, the sound of the truck's horn triggered in Fred's mind, the biblical story of Peter's denial, his mother had told him years ago. As Fred thought about it, he turned his head toward the window so the driver could not see the tears that had formed in Fred's eyes. However, he was alive.

# CHAPTER 9

## *Mattie*

On the morning following the first Tuesday after the first Monday of November 2008, Mattie Meyers was still amazed, in much the same manner her great-grandmother Adline Tedder was amazed a couple of years after the Civil War ended. She was not so amazed that this nation had just elected Barack Obama as its first African-American President. She was amazed that she was alive to see it!

Mattie walked across her kitchen—her office—and poured some oatmeal into a large bowl with a little water, and placed it into her microwave oven, something else with what she was amazed. Mattie was born and raised in a small house in Durham, North Carolina, during the Great Depression. The home where she grew up did not have electricity until she was near an adult, and never had a telephone until well after she left home. Microwave ovens, computers, cellular telephones were all things she would have never thought possible as a child, much less ever own.

If you asked Mattie, she would tell you that she thought of her upbringing during the Depression as being dirt poor. The fact that her father worked for the same fabric mill every day while one-fourth of the country's population of all races and ethnicities were unemployed, did not quite register to Mattie as a child. In fact, they were surely much better off than most African-Americans at the time, as well as a large percentage of White-Americans.

For instance, her father and mother owned—or at least owned the mortgage on—the home they were raised, when many families were homeless in that era of our nation's history.

Mattie's uncle had built their small three-room home in the early twenties prior to the onset of the Great Depression, and her father had secured a home loan that he was able to pay each month. Her father was able to pay the mortgage, as well as clothe and feed his family from the wages he made from his job at a Durham fabric mill, employed there continuously until his death in the early 1950s.

Consequently, Mattie, her brother Fred Jr., and their two older sisters never went to bed hungry, while many stood in soup lines at the time, although there was not much left for anything else.

To that issue, Mattie's mother, Julia Douglas Burton, in addition to taking care of the house and children, sold eggs from the chickens she raised, and vegetables from her garden in the side and backyard of their Durham home.

In fact, it was the extra money that her mother made from her little home business enterprises that allowed the Burtons in the mid-1930s to purchase the installation of running water and inside plumbing, including a bathtub and an indoor commode, all considered luxuries in that era and locale.

Ironically, if we were living in today's value set, Mattie's mother could have provided much more. Julia had a college education from Orangeburg State College, an African-American college established just after the Civil War in South Carolina. She occasionally had worked as a substitute teacher in Durham's Black school system and could have worked as a regular schoolteacher in that school system if her husband would have allowed such a thing.

Even Mattie's grandfather at the turn of the century and a mere 40 years out of Reconstruction was a college graduate, with a degree in divinity from a college in Missouri that he proudly displayed on his wall until his death.

Good blood was on her father's side of the Burton family as well. Her father's uncle was an educator, who went on to become the superintendent of Durham's African-American school system for a few years. Both sides of Mattie's family stressed the importance of education and hard work as the means to success in life.

The reality was that Mattie's family was not dirt poor, just poor, but far ahead of most people that surrounded her life in Durham, whether she realized it or not, and she certainly sported a good set of genes.

Mattie would tell you that she never realized how well she and others had it living in a larger city in the segregated South until 1947, when she stepped off the train in her new home of Fresno, California. She would say that she was shocked to see the large number of African-Americans living in abject poverty conditions, in stark contrast to the small numbers of educated Black people in the area, so small, you could count the African-American college graduates on one hand with a finger or two left over.

That difference had to do with the great migration of blacks out of the South during the Great Depression. Like depicted for Whites in John Steinbeck's *Grapes of Wrath*, the fertile fields of the San Joaquin Valley also held a promise for downtrodden African-Americans, to work harvesting the bounty of the agricultural fields and orchards. It was the attraction of back-breaking farm labor and an occasional paycheck, not the dream of riches for the Black migrants.

As Mattie ate her breakfast, she did think to herself that she had caught a lot of good breaks during her life, or to her thinking, was blessed by the Lord with good fortune.

She almost died as an infant, apparently from an allergic reaction. As she grew older, that sensitivity increased, especially to milk-related products. As an adult, she became hypersensitive to many chemicals and foods.

Mattie often thought it is funny how things work sometimes. By the nature of her allergies, she could only eat simple foods that are naturally low in fats and bad cholesterol, and just about nothing processed with modern food-production methods. Exactly the kinds of foods recommended by health experts in promoting healthy living and longevity. Her limited diet as a result turned out to be something that she felt prolonged her life and health.

She thought about the day when she was about twelve, her parents asked her if she might be interested in living with, and helping Miss Fanny Rosser, a fairly wealthy Black businesswoman who lived near the college, in exchange for help in providing a college education. This was a common practice during those days.

Both fulfilled their ends of the agreement; Mattie worked hard and studied well, and Miss Rosser sent Mattie to North Carolina College (now North Carolina Central University, Durham), where she graduated with a Bachelor of Science degree in Biology and went to work at the Black Lincoln Hospital in Durham.

She married well, she thought. While employed at the hospital, she met a young doctor from California doing his practical training, and a year later they were married and, on a train, heading to Fresno, California, a place she would call home until her death about 70 years later.

Mattie finished her breakfast, cleaned off the table and started to wash the few dishes by hand, as she continued her morning musings. She thought about how well she and her husband, Dr. Earl R. Meyers, did during the first 15 or so years of their marriage.

Earl Meyers' background was completely different from Mattie. Earl's father, Louis Meyers, was in the scrap metal business during the Great Depression, the perfect kind of business to be in during a severe economic downturn, when manufactured materials are in short supply.

As a result, Louis Meyers did very well, both during the Great Depression, and especially during and after World War II when metals were in short supply and Louis knew where to find and recycle them at a nice profit. By the end of World War II, Earl's father was arguably about the most financially successful Black man in the San Joaquin Valley.

Although Earl Meyers was not the first African-American physician to practice in the Fresno area, he was the first in the modern, post-World War II baby boom era, the previous being out of practice for at least five years. There were only a few physicians in the area that would accept any minority patients at all when Dr. Meyers started his medical practice.

Together, Mattie and Earl built a remarkably successful medical practice, later a medical center and opened doors for other minority medical professionals. Earl of course provided the healthcare, and Mattie handled the business matters. Both she and her husband were active in civil rights starting in the 1950s, maybe a little more so for Mattie.

She was the president of Fresno's NAACP chapter in 1960, at the apex of the Civil Rights Movement. During the early sixties, she marched in the South right alongside Dr. Martin Luther King, and later, she marched with him when he came to Fresno to call attention to racial discrimination within California housing.

She worked in local politics, both as a Democratic Party loyalist, and in 1963, as a serious candidate for city mayor. She was the first Black woman, the first woman for that matter to do such a thing that gained her some attention with women in general, especially during the mid-sixties with the emerging new ideas regarding gender roles.

She returned to graduate school in the early sixties, earning a master's degree in education, and began a career in teaching after a divorce from her one and only husband. All during this time, she raised five children, four boys and one girl.

This year, she was working on a book about her life that she hoped to publish in the next few months. Her hope was that her memoirs would provide inspiration for her grandchildren, and their children that followed.

It was late morning when her doorbell rang. She knew it would be her daughter because she had called the night before, saying she would be bringing a young man over for her to meet. It took a lot of pleading from her daughter before she agreed. Mattie did not like any changes in her carefully established routine. However, Mattie agreed, and here they were at the door.

She went to the door and called out, "Who is it?" Mattie lived alone and was always incredibly careful.

"It's your daughter, Gayle," her daughter responded. Gayle quickly added, "With Frank. The man I told you about."

Recognizing the voice with the correct information, she opened the door and looked at the young man standing next to her daughter, paused a moment, and then said as a matter of fact, "You must be Fred's son."

Her response did not give away the fact that she was quite shocked with the visitor standing on her porch. Her daughter had made no mention that she was going to bring over a relative that no one knew existed. She started laughing. "Well, am I correct?"

Everyone except for Frank was laughing. Frank just stood there for a moment with a nervous look on his face and replied, "Yes, ma'am. Well, we really don't know that for sure," Frank nervously stated.

"Well, *we* know you're unmistakably Fred's son. You look exactly like him when he was your age," Mattie stated. She motioned them in, sat them in the small living room area adjacent to the front door entryway.

Frank surveyed the room. Frank was good at sizing people up by what they kept around them. He could see the home was clean, but not spotless. The living room area contained old furniture, maybe from the fifties; old, but well-kept over the years. There were a few pictures on a table, a couple of plaques and pictures on a wall, and no television.

This was obviously a formal reception area, where Mattie sized people up. Frank smiled… a bit impressed. He concluded this woman was smart, creative, accomplished, proud, and accustomed to being in control.

Mattie continued, "Just how you managed to be here all this time, and no one knew of you is beyond me. "

"Actually," Frank said, "I am not from Fresno. I am just here on business this week. I live in Portland, Oregon, originally from Bend. I just started coming to Fresno on a regular basis about a year ago when I got a new position at work. I've been to Fresno three times in the past year, and a couple of other times in the two previous years."

Mattie took in what Frank said, and replied, "Maybe you aren't Fred's son after all. I don't know if Fred ever spent too much time in Oregon, beyond just passing through."

Gayle, seated in an old wooden rocking chair, said, "There's more to it, Mom. Tell her, Frank."

Gayle was getting excited, speaking very quickly she said, "Mom, Frank's mother met Fred in Sacramento."

Mattie cut her daughter off, saying in a stern voice, "Gayle, let Frank tell the story." She waited a moment and then said in a sweet-sounding voice, "Go on, Frank."

"Okay, Mrs. Meyers. Just before I was born, my mom was living in Sacramento. My mom told me of a 'Fred,' but she never mentioned anything about him being African-American. Those things make me think we are talking about different people, Mrs. Meyers. When I was born, she said my father was Fred Langton, not Fred Burton, who lived in Sacramento," said Frank.

Mattie was smiling as she slowly shook her head. "You appear to be a very intelligent young man, Frank," Mattie replied. "You do know Fred's full name was Fred Langston Burton, right?"

Frank nodded his head.

"Surely you can see when you put the first part of Fred's middle name together with the last part of '*Burton,*' his last name, you come up with '*Langton.*' Now Frank, I just figured that out in two seconds. It seems pretty obvious your mother did not want you to find too much information about your father."

"You're probably right, Mrs. Meyers. I too figured that much out." Frank went on. "My mom did tell me the story about how she met my dad." Frank told Mattie and Gayle the entire story about how she got to Sacramento, and met his father, skipping the part about his mother's life before she moved to California.

When he told the part about how she left Sacramento, without saying a word to Fred about leaving, and made sure he could never find her again, Mattie responded.

"Well, Fred must have told her that he was a Black man," Mattie simply stated. "I can see how that might have been a little too much for her to handle."

"No, no… my mom is not like that," he blurted out. "My mom is a fair person and always told me to treat everyone as who they are… she's not a racist."

"Frank, I am sure your mom is a very *fair* woman, without any ill intent. I must say, Frank, I think that most people really want to do the right thing," Mattie explained. "We are all children of the Lord, created in His image."

"I also know that when it comes down to a mother and her child, *fair* or *the right thing* has nothing to do with anything when it involves her child's welfare. I think your mother was just looking out for what she thought would make your life the least complicated, Frank, whether I agree or not." Mattie then said, "Please, go on and tell me more, Frank."

Frank finished talking about the hypothetical discussion he had with his girlfriend the previous night.

Mattie chuckled. "I would not take what she said as her final answer, Frank. That woman has not really considered anything yet. It will not become real to her until you tell her what you just told me. Although I would imagine what she said is probably going to be her final answer if you ever tell her the truth." She then asked Frank, "Have you asked you mother?"

"Are you kidding?" Frank sat straight up. "I am not going to have a discussion with my mom about this unless I am pretty convinced. She's gone through enough in her life, Mrs. Meyers."

Mattie said, "Okay. Let's talk about convince. Here are the facts, Frank." She began to rattle off each point as if she were a lawyer, listing out her contentions to a group of jurors.

**Mattie:** "Your father lived in California, correct?"
**Frank:** "Yes."
**Mattie:** "Your father was a truck driver, correct?"

**Frank:** "Yes, he was, according to my mom."
**Mattie:** "Your father ran away from his home in North Carolina when he was a child. Is that right?"
**Frank:** "Yes, it is."
**Mattie:** "He acted like a cowboy, worked as a cowboy, and he knew horses, right?"
**Frank:** "Yes."
**Mattie:** "He told a story to your mother about working for the Hearst Castle Ranch?"
**Frank:** "Yep. I see where this is going, Mrs. Meyers."

Then Gayle added with a laugh, "And you look just like him, Frank. That's enough for me, Cuz'." Gayle could not stop laughing.

Mattie added, "Of course, you do. These are exactly the same things that are true about my brother. You know what I think, Frank? I think there are few questions about it. Fred Langston Burton is probably your father." Mattie said this as a fact. "I don't think you need a paternity test or anything like that to prove it. Although I guess that is the only other thing you could do if you need to prove what you already know. That stuff is pretty accurate these days from what I've read. Me, or Gayle I am sure, would be willing to get you a blood sample for one of those new DNA tests if you'd like."

Mattie continued, "The question really is what do you do with this information, and how do you go about your life from here. The fact is, even if true, you'll still be Frank." She laughed.

"Mrs. Meyers," Frank replied, "I don't understand why your brother went through such great pains to hide all this. He must have really thought he had a different father, or that your mother was Indian like he told those other people."

She chuckled again. "I don't think so, Frank. I really cannot see how he could have believed that. Fred would have known better. Fred has an extraordinarily rich family history of which he was very much aware, even at the age he left home. "

"Frank," said Mattie, "why don't you come into the kitchen and let me fix you and Gayle something to eat? I'll explain why the idea that Fred didn't know is so absurd while I am making lunch."

# CHAPTER 10

## *Tedder versus Tedder*

Gayle, sounding like an excited little girl, replied, "Okay, Mama. Frank, come in here and get some of my mother's cooking."

Mattie guided her daughter and Frank into her kitchen. It was obvious to Frank that this area was where she spent most of her time. There was a table in the middle of the small room, with enough room for three or four people to sit comfortably. In the middle of the table was a jar filled with pencils and pens, and a reading light near one of the chairs. On one counter, there was a small television next to her telephone. She had rows of bills, business statements, and notes, all lined neatly in rows on the same counter. The kitchen part looked to be coincidental.

After she seated Gayle and Frank, she walked over to what was meant to be a dining area that she had arranged and furnished more akin an office. The room included a small desk with a computer, and some short file cabinets against the wall, next to which were a couple of storage containers meant to store paper documents.

Frank thought, *This woman is not into entertaining a slew of friends.*

Mattie took the top off one of the storage containers, and picked out a thick brown envelope, from which she pulled out a photo that she handed to the now seated Frank.

The photo she handed Frank was an eight-by-ten black-and-white photo of a white complected woman with black hair and light-colored eyes, obviously taken in a studio. She said, "That's my mother, Julia Burton. She is both the mother of Fred and I."

Frank squinted a little as he examined the photo and asked a little puzzled, "Was she white?" Frank thought there was nothing that looked black about the woman in the picture.

"I am going to tell you all about it if you give me a minute, Frank." She walked over to the freezer and started to pull some containers from her freezer as she continued speaking.

"Frank, I can't eat like most people. I have very severe allergies and I have to make everything I eat from scratch. I almost died as a little girl from an allergic reaction to milk and it got much worse as I grew older. I think I would be dead now if I did not learn how to prepare the foods I eat in an extremely basic manner. I make everything once a week from scratch, and then freeze it for the microwave."

Frank, for the first time in his life, upon hearing someone that seemed to have some empathy with his own problems with food, commented, "You know, Mrs. Meyers, I have food allergies that also include milk. I must be extremely careful, especially when I am eating out. Most of the time, I just get hives all over and maybe an upset stomach."

Mattie, between warming the food containers in the microwave, stopped and looked at Frank extremely hard and said, "Frank, if your doctor has not told you, don't fool around with your allergies. You can have a reaction that can kill you, Frank. You're likely going to have to learn to deal with food as I have."

Mattie then changed back to the original subject. "Frank, you were asking if the woman in that picture, my mother Julia, is White."

Mattie pushed the start button that produced a "beep," and then turned toward Frank. "The answer to that question is no. She was very African-American and would quickly correct you if you were to suggest otherwise." Frank picked up the picture and was staring intently when Mattie added with a little laugh, "You think you see someone familiar, don't you, Frank?"

Frank said, "I have to admit that at first glance, I can see a little resemblance. But she definitely resembles you, and the picture of your brother Fred the man at the restaurant showed me."

Mattie handed him three more old black-and-white photos, this time of a very dark-skinned man. She said, "Well, that's Fred's father, Fred Senior... my dad. He was an enormously proud man, Frank. I remember when he'd come home from work, every day, take off his work clothes, and put on a clean suit with a tie.

"I remember when I was a child, he'd sometimes take me over to the North Carolina College, the Black college in Durham, to hear some eloquent speaker of the time such as The Reverend, and later, Congressman Adam Clayton Powell Jr. of New York, or Dr. Benjamin Mays of Morehouse College, or NAACP Chief Walter White, Roy Wilkins, and others. From these gatherings, he would come home and discuss with the family the message of the day.

"He did not have a great deal of formal education, but he felt education was the most important thing for his children," Mattie added. "He'd take me on educational walks on occasions, to places like the city water treatment plant. Then he would explain how it worked."

Next, she handed Frank an incredibly old picture of a family sitting outdoors. It measured about four inches high and six inches wide, mounted on a piece of crumbling cardboard. The picture had many scratches, but it was clearly an old original photograph.

"That, Frank, is my grandfather, Grandpa Jim, my mother's father. I was fortunate to have been able to know my Grandpa Jim," Mattie said. "I remember he was quiet, and he'd toss me a nickel for doing something like washing his coveralls he liked to wear. We washed our clothes by hand in those days, you know."

The microwave chimed, and Mattie removed the dish, and put another into the oven and pushed the start button. She turned back to Frank.

Mattie smiled. "Well, visiting my Grandpa Jim was my greatest joy when I was a child, Frank. He lived a half-block down the street from our home, right across the street from W. G. Pearson Elementary School. That school's name is in honor of my father's great uncle. I attended this elementary school when I was a child, Frank."

Mattie seemed to reflect for a moment. "After my grandmother died, I remember Grandpa seemed lonely. As a girl, I looked forward to visiting with him."

"You see, Frank," Mattie continued, "my grandfather, James Tedder, was the son of a white plantation farmer. He made a striking and handsome appearance with his tall, slender frame, straight black hair, keen facial features, and fair skin.

"He was a talented and learned man, Frank, who graduated from college in St. Louis, Missouri, with a theology degree. I remember there was a diploma that Grandpa Jim, kept on his wall that I would see when I visited at his house. By the way, Frank, Grandpa Jim is the name I called him as a child. He married my grandmother, Julia Mae Douglas of Society Hill, South Carolina."

Pointing at each person in the picture as she spoke, Mattie continued, "They had five children: my mother Julia, Ailene, Annette, James Jr., and Douglas. My Aunt Annette is not in this picture because she died in her early childhood. Because of what I recall hearing when I was a child, I now think she died of the same kind of allergy-related issues I have.

"Both Grandpa Jim and my Grandma Julia came from families of many siblings and both of their fathers were white plantation farmers married to African-American women. Marriages of their kind are still little acknowledged in American history but were more common than what many think, Frank.

"Obviously, my grandfather was a minister. My mother said that he became a *changed* man after fighting and losing a battle with South Carolina lawmakers for the large acreage of land left by his father. "

Frank asked, "Is that why you said that your mother was so adamant about not allowing anyone to think she was anything but a Black woman?"

"That is absolutely correct, Frank," Mattie responded. "You see, she was probably about fourteen or fifteen when that case was settled, and the government took their land away. If you can imagine her, my mother's brothers and sisters, their uncles and cousins all growing up with their dreams and aspirations for their children's success all but assured, and then have those dreams snatched from them, twelve years after the fact."

Mattie pointed at the young woman that was standing in the old family photograph and said, "My mother, that's her about the time this all happened. She said that she saw it as nothing more than a land grab by a bunch of greedy Whites that she could not forget because of what it did to the entire family, especially my grandfather. No, my mother saw nothing glorious about being mistaken for a White woman. Fred Jr. knew all of this... we all did.

"You see, Frank, although my grandfather went to Tallahassee, Florida, and obtained the proof of marriage, the racial discrimination laws of inheritance for children born from a mother of African descent deprived my grandfather of land his father meant for him. After a bitter and losing legal battle, my grandfather moved his family from Society Hill, South Carolina, to Durham, North Carolina, so that his children could get a good education. The whole family had to adjust.

"As the story goes, my mother and her sister were both in college after their land was taken. After leaving Claflin and Orangeburg State College, my mother and her sister matriculated into North Carolina College at Durham. Her two brothers went to Hillside High School. My grandfather and grandmother got jobs at Liggett and Myers Tobacco Factory, considered good jobs at that time."

Frank had a look of being in deep thought while he was listening. When Mattie finished, he stated, "You know, Mrs. Meyers, that story is very different than what I was taught about Black people, especially in the South." Frank sounded very unconvinced. "Some of what you just told me is really a little unbelievable."

"Maybe, Frank," replied Mattie. "But it is the truth. People here in the West and in the northern United States don't really know that much about what it was like in the South when I was a child. In Durham, the city in North Carolina where I grew up had a rich African-American community.

"I remember one day, or maybe a number of days that I vividly recall when I was a little girl, my mother would take me and my sisters, Margaret and Clara, on long walks. Well, walking was our only transportation... at least the only transportation we could afford.

"First, we'd walk about a half-mile to what was called the Hayti shopping section, which consisted of many businesses owned or operated by African-Americans. There were restaurants, barber shops, drycleaners, banks, grocery stores, pharmacies, ice cream parlors, service station, lodges, beauty shops, Saint Joseph African-American Episcopal Methodist Church, White Rock Baptist Church, doctors and lawyers' offices. Some were owned by whites, but many of these businesses were both Black owned and operated.

"You see, Frank, it had to be that way. The Jim Crow laws said that Black people and white people had to have separate, but equal facilities. It was definitely separate, but in reality, not very equal. But we, the African-American community, tried to make it as equal as we could at the time.

"So, when we walked through the Black sections of town, on each side there were large, beautiful, palatial two-story homes, owned by the more prosperous African-Americans. The largest building in this section was the Royal Knights of King David, three stories tall. Next door was the Teachers Home that housed African-American teachers who taught during the school year and went to their homes in different cities when school was out.

"My mother and I, along with my sisters, would walk further north on Fayetteville Street into the next section that was called Mexico. There was a hosiery mill, a long red brick building where large numbers of African-Americans worked.

"On the opposite side of the street were the railroad tracks and the African-American branch of the City library. The next block going north had a theater, pool hall, another drug store, hotel, the Regal Theater, Liggett and Myers and Lucky Strike Tobacco Factories, where mostly African-Americans worked.

"Then, about a half-mile northeast was the uptown section consisting of Durham's City Hall, classy stores, the jail, and other buildings which catered to the entire population of the city and carried on all the major political, civic, and businesses of the city.

"Finally, Frank, I remember thinking it was odd that in this predominantly white hub was a three-story brick building, the North Carolina Mutual Life Insurance Company, completely owned and operated by African-Americans, one of the most successful Black-owned companies in the country."

Mattie reached into the envelope and pulled out a picture that appeared to be printed from a computer. "That's a picture of the North Carolina Mutual building, Frank. The woman who I lived with, and who sent me to college, worked there."

"Again, Mrs. Meyers, you are telling me things that I never knew about the South," said Frank. "Where I grew up in Bend, there were some Black people who worked at the University and in the schools, but not very many. Until I met David Brewer, my boss, I did not know any really successful businesspeople who were African-American."

"Like I said, Frank, if you are not from the South, in a lot of cases people just don't know about it," Mattie explained. "And Frank, that business about my great-grandfather who once was a slave owner being married to my great-grandmother was not an aberration. Both southern White families and Black families alike know all about stories like this that they know are true. They just don't talk about it very much, or they say it is just a lie."

Frank then asked, "Well, how do you know that the story about your great-grandfather is a real story and not just something that's been handed down, that may, or may not be true?"

"Because, Frank, my oldest granddaughter, Sharon, Gayle's daughter, did some research and found some of the White family members who talked about it with her. They, too, knew all about it. They also directed her to a court case that told just about everything that you ever wanted to know, all written down in legal writings that include names, dates, and who did what with who." Mattie started laughing and recounted the story about her great-grandfather and his wife Adline.

Mattie told Frank about her grandfather, and apparently Frank's great-grandfather, James Tedder. She told him that James Tedder was the father of her mother Julia. She explained how his life had also abruptly changed.

She said to Frank, "At the beginning of the twentieth century, the former white slave-owner, my great-grandfather, William Tedder Jr., was an old man, his wife Adline, my great-grandmother, passed 15 years earlier, and she was nearly twenty years younger than him.

"William Tedder had nine children, and his four oldest boys got the most attention from him personally, because he was advanced in age, well into his forties when he began this family with his new wife, the former Black slave Adline, about two years after the end of the Civil War.

"The four oldest sons, my great-uncles Augustus, James, Willie, and Samuel, were all born within about five years, right after the Civil War. And all four worked closely with their father who taught them how to farm and maintain a farm business.

"My great-grandfather William controlled more than five hundred acres of farmland, raising both livestock that included pigs, and crops. It was more than adequate to provide his family with a wonderfully comfortable income for his eventual family of nine children.

"All the boys got a full public education that meant they had gone through about the sixth grade… they could read, write, and knew basic math. This was the top of the new primary education system of the time. James, my Grandpa Jim, later went to college in Saint Louis, where he received a college degree in divinity. Grandpa Jim returned to his home in Society Hill, where he became a Methodist minister, along with farming about forty acres of land."

Frank interrupted, "How do you know this is true?"

Mattie replied, "Because, Frank, my granddaughter, Sharon, found the actual court case that took their land away. It's all there in the court documents, spelled out in black and white. We knew all about it when we were kids. Sharon just confirmed what we had always been told."

"Okay." Frank shifted in his seat. "So, what happened next?"

Mattie continued. "Although interracial marriages were illegal in South Carolina at the time, William took his wife to Florida, where the law was different, and legally married his wife Adline. When William died in 1905, he left a clear legal will that divided any remaining land among his boys, and legally solidified to his children any property previously sold or gifted to them.

"Upon William's death, the distribution of property went without any hitch. Everyone in and around Society Hill knew William and his albeit unusual, but apparently legitimate family, and acknowledged that he was married to Adline, regardless if they agreed with the marriage or not. So, William's Black children, especially the four oldest boys, went on to live comfortably, if not prosperous lifestyles for some years to come.

"Now that picture you're holding, Frank, is my mother's family, James and Julia Tedder." Mattie pointed at a tall and very pretty young woman in the picture. "My mother, Julia, was the eldest of James' four children by several years. Julia was a few years older than her remaining two brothers and sister.

"Like Fred, Mama was exceptionally light skinned, had straight un-coarse hair, and blue eyes. She could have easily been mistaken for being White, a strikingly beautiful young woman by the beauty standards of the time.

"My mother was very much her father's daughter. I believe Grandpa Jim was most impressed with how bright and talented she was. Mama, at an early age, played piano and sang at her father's church. She learned the Bible as well as anyone, and she loved to tell biblical stories, and taught in her father's Sunday school.

"Her family, including her uncles that lived nearby, owned horses that Mama regularly rode. She went to Claflin College, the oldest college for African-Americans in South Carolina. She was educated to the point where she could teach school. Remember, Frank, the education system was different in those times."

At this point, Mattie paused in the story she was telling Frank and said, "So, Frank, you can see how your great-grandfather's family would make you proud. If you take away skin color, wouldn't you agree that your great-great-grandparents represent the best in hard work and devotion to their children?"

"Yes, Mrs. Meyers, I can see that," said Frank. "They sound like any other positive-seeking family."

"And Frank," Mattie replied, "as far as I know, there were never any stories about stereotypical claims about stealing, going to jail, or any of the kinds of things people tried to apply to African-Americans, especially at that time. Although, there were not so happy things that occurred, to be sure.

"In the case of my mother, she lived what most would say was a very charmed lifestyle for the times she was growing up. There was only one snag," Mattie said as she continued the story.

Mattie continued, "William Tedder, my mother's grandfather, before the onset of the Civil War had successfully raised another family of five children with a previous wife, a White woman named Jimima Griggs Tedder, who died some years earlier. The children from this marriage were all adults, and well into their adult lives when William married Adline sometime after the beginning of the Civil War.

"William's marriage to Adline never sat right with his first family. They pretty much ignored him for the rest of his life. So, when William died, conspicuously absent from any distribution of his estate were the children from his first marriage. Like I said earlier, the people in and around Society Hill knew of the strained relationship he had with his White children and accepted the idea that he would not leave them anything beyond what they had already been given.

"There was a good reason why it never sat right, Frank. The year after William Tedder died, one of William's children from his first marriage challenged William Tedder's will on behalf of the rest of his White descendants.

"It turns out that this was not the first time that the Tedders were in court regarding the family fortune. Most of William Tedder's holdings came directly from his first wife Jimima's family. The estate begins with William and Mary Griggs, the aunt of William Tedder's first wife Jimima.

"Prior to the Civil War, William Griggs owned about six hundred acres of land in Darlington County, South Carolina, along with 27 slaves and various personal property items. William and Mary were childless. Upon William's death in 1856, the property went to his wife Mary. In compliance with the will, the property and business interest should have remained with Mary until her death. As specified, upon Mary's death, the estate was slated for distribution to Mary's nieces and nephews that included the niece, Jimima Griggs.

"At the time that William Tedder's first wife, Jimima, died in 1859, the number of slaves within the estate of Mary Griggs had increased to 32, three of whom were sold prior to the end of the Civil War. The short version is that upon Mary's death in 1873, as a result of a business deal between Mary Griggs and William Tedder, William ended up with about one-third of Mary's estate, and at least one member of Jimima Griggs' family was not happy with the split, so she took William Tedder to court and eventually lost.

"According to the court case my youngest son found, the 1881 South Carolina appeal of *Moody v. Tedder* finally resolved the case, pretty much in favor of William Tedder, who ended up keeping his inheritance intact. Add to it the fact that William Tedder and his Black family were living, literally next door to his White children and their relatives, added to the tension.

"So, with the death of William Tedder in 1905, William Tedder's land at first transferred to the Black children in the manner he had willed. The will was challenged by the White children the next year, but the lower court in Darlington struck the case down, and the Black children kept the property. Keep in mind, these were courts controlled by the white community of South Carolina. They ruled twice, unequivocally in the Black Tedders' favor."

Mattie, continuing the story she was telling Frank, said, "But in 1917, twelve years after William Tedder's death, this simmering tension ended up in front of the South Carolina Supreme Court, Frank. It was not over by a long shot.

"My mother was about 12 years old, a young adult really in those days," Mattie said. She went on. "In 1917, Furman Tedder, the White son of William and Jimima, managed to get this case heard by the South Carolina Supreme Court."

"So, what happened?" Frank asked. "Did they get to keep the land?"

"Well, Frank, if you can be a little patient and let me finish the story, you are about to find out."

# CHAPTER 11

## Gus, James, Willie, and Samuel

Mattie served lunch. It was simple but tasty. Some chicken that she served with rice, along with a leafy vegetable that Frank was unfamiliar with, but it was particularly good. When he asked what it was, Mattie explained they were collard greens. Everything she served had already been prepared and frozen. She warmed everything in the microwave.

As they ate lunch, she continued telling Frank about her grandfather.

In October of 1918, Mattie's grandfather, a very dejected James Tedder, sat on his front porch looking over the more than 500 acres of land he and his brothers had called their own for their entire lives up until this day, the land that had provided his family with a very good lifestyle since their births. A few minutes earlier, his daughter Julia, the oldest of his children, had hugged him with tears in her eyes and left to join the rest of the family inside the only home they had known.

James would have told you flat out that he was scared regarding the future of his family. He would also tell you that he was terribly angry. He was angry about the conspiracy that brought him to this day... angry with God Himself. As a Methodist minister, a college graduate with a bachelor's degree in divinity, and a man of intense faith in the Lord, he tried to look at his current plight through the experiences of Job.

Unlike Job, he was a having a problem accepting the Lord's will in this matter. Like David in his confrontation with Goliath, his faith had told him the Lord's will would prevail. Realistically, he knew that he and his brothers were living at the height of Jim Crow and the Ku Klux Klan. He knew the chances of them prevailing in a South Carolina court, against the interests of a bunch of greedy men -White men- were nil at best. But until today, he had expected for the Lord to take care of him and his family.

The beginning of this end started about a year or so earlier when the South Carolina Supreme Court announced the ruling in the appeal that emanated from their inheritance case, "Tedder v. Tedder." This land dispute propagated by the white children of "Old Man William" Tedder had been going on for more than ten years. Several court proceedings took place over the years, and in each, the Black children—James and his three brothers—had prevailed. Therefore, all things being the same, it seemed to James that with the Lord's will, they would prevail in this state Supreme Court case.

A few weeks prior, James and his brothers had gathered at the oldest brother, Augustus' (Gus), home when they heard the latest bad news. The meeting took place on a Sunday evening after church, after they had all eaten and Gus' children were put to bed.

Augustus was the oldest, and like his brothers was tall, having sharp features like their father. He said, "Well, I went through Daddy's papers a couple of months ago and found the marriage certificate."

Willie added, "You already told us that, Gus. What's your point? They already explained that we can't give evidence to the appeal."

Gus said, "The point is that last week I personally took those papers, including the marriage certificate, to our lawyers in Darlington to put with the rest of the case. I am thinking what we gonna do after the appeal. You rememba they said they are gonna be concerned with what wasn't in Daddy's probate hearing when he died twelve years ago?"

"Yeah. I see where you're goin' with this, Gus," answered James. "It is likely we're going to have to go back to court after the appeal and show proof that Mama and Daddy were married, and that was not in the first hearing because nobody said they weren't. Everyone agreed that they were married."

James added, "But they also said that the South Carolina Supreme Court may not recognize the marriage no hows because marriages between a Colored and White is not legal in the state. But I agree with you that we should have everything we may need."

James quickly said, "Then that's it. We got the marriage certificate and that should be all we need."

Augustus, raising his voice, said, "No! That ain't it. You rememba they said that a marriage certificate is not enough, and they probably won't look at it no ways. They gonna want to hear from someone who can say they saw 'em married. Most of all them folks is dead… been dead for years."

After a moment of silence, Samuel, the youngest of the brothers, said in an irritated tone, "That don't make no sense no how. The paper says they were married, all legal."

To that, James replied, "There are still some folks who are still alive that knew Mama and Daddy. I think we are way in front of this. First, we've got to hear what the court has to say. Mayhaps the certificate is enough and mayhaps it is not. What I know is that this is a matter of right, and I know the Lord will see that what is right prevails."

Willie, a businessman, added the last words before the meeting broke up that evening. He said, "Just in case, I am going to make sure we know who might be able to say they saw Mama and Daddy married, and that we got as many papers as we can find, just in case."

He laughed and added, "I want the Lord to have as much to work with as possible."

Willie's last comment lightened things up a little, and they all left before heading home.

As it turned out, several weeks later the four stunned brothers found themselves right back in Gus' home, trying to make sense out of the condescending ruling from the South Carolina Supreme Court. Moreover, they were left trying to figure out how to address the "Show Cause" summons requiring the brothers to present evidence why their property should not be stripped from them to comply with the court ruling.

"No… they say that because Colored and Whites cannot be married in South Carolina, the marriage papers from Florida are against the law here and mean nothing," answered Gus.

"It still don't make no sense. Everybody knows that Mama and Daddy were married, including those crackers over yonder that just want to take our land," Samuel responded. "Hard to believe they even got Daddy's blood."

James jumped back in, "I think Samuel may be right. We got a whole lot of people, *white people*, who say they'll tell the court Mama and Daddy were married. We are his children."

Finally, Willie, the businessperson of the bunch, delivered his conclusion. "You know, the deck is stacked against us. Them boys got good lawyers and the whole lot, and there ain't no tellin' what them old White folks who knew Mama and Daddy will say about their marriage. But I declare, I think I got a good handle on what them boys will have to say. We are living in a time when anything that anyone wants from coloreds is all but a foregone conclusion.

"Try to get all the papers you can before we gotta go to Darlington next month, all the people that can vouch for us, and pray to the Lord." Then Willie added, "But I think things are gonna change."

It occurred to James that his younger brother Willie might be right. A few weeks after the meeting, James heard of a Negro photographer passing through Society Hill. Although a little expensive, he decided to have the photographer take a picture of the family at their farm home.

The next afternoon, the photographer arrived. His wife Julia Mae had already told her two daughters to be dressed and ready to take a picture with the family. James' oldest son James Jr. had dressed himself, and he and his sisters were impatiently waiting for their mother to get their youngest son Douglas ready.

Finally, they were all ready and went outside along the side of their wood-framed house where the photographer had set up his camera. It was a bright day, and there was a breeze blowing across the landscape. A shuttered window behind Aileen kept swinging open, and James finally went over and tied it down with a piece of string.

James sat back down on a step, and the photographer, catching them a little off guard, immediately said, "Okay. Y'all hold still."

For what seemed like a long few seconds, no one moved. The breeze kept blowing Aileen's straight hair, and young Julia's dress. Then the photographer said, "Okay. That's it."

As it turned out, Willie was right as they all found out the next month when the Court delivered its decision.

In terms of the marriage of Adline and William, the court decided that despite any testimony that showed that William and Adline were living as husband and wife, the marriage of a white man to a colored woman was, in the court's words, immoral and illegal by state law, common law and yes, even by God. There was no mention of any kind of marriage certificates or evidence stemming from census records.

The ruling said that any agreements that the children may have had with their father, unless they could show that they had substantial investments to indicate they had purchased the asset, there could not be any other transfer of property to the Black illegitimate children over the legitimate White children.

In short, the Supreme Court decision totally reversed the lower court ruling that had originally allowed the transfer of William Tedder's property to the children of Adline and William, affecting some 340 acres of land, valued at the time at about 20,000 dollars, a considerable sum in 1917.

Only Willie Tedder ended up with a small amount of land, about thirty acres or so, because he was later able to show documents attesting to a number of payments, he had made for a parcel of land that, in essence, had a mortgage when the agreement with his father deeded the land to him. William and Adline's other children lost the remaining land because of this decision.

A few days later, an envelope arrived that contained five copies of the photograph that James had arranged a month earlier. James would later give each of his children one of the photos. As it turned out, this was the only snapshot of the life they once had, and now lost.

Mattie pointed at one of those remaining photographs as she continued her conversation with Frank, nearly a hundred years later.

"I remember all of my great-uncles very well," Mattie said to Frank. "In fact, I can remember Fred and I taking a ride to South Carolina with my Uncle Douglas when I was a young girl and visiting with my uncle Willie at his store. I remember both my great uncles Augustus and Willie as appearing very prosperous for Black people at the time. So, those two apparently figured out a way to make it after that catastrophe of 1917.

"My grandfather, *Grandpa Jim*, was a different story," Mattie added. "My mother said that her father was a broken man after that and was never the same. He moved to Durham, North Carolina, where he and my grandmother took jobs at the tobacco factory. He never preached again."

Frank replied, "That is sad, Mrs. Meyers."

"I think Grandpa Jim expected the Lord to take care of him. The way Grandpa Jim thought He should take care of him and his family," Mattie said. "Sometimes we don't understand that the Lord is painting on a much larger canvas, Frank, and it's hard to see our place on it.

"As for my mother, she was very close to Grandpa Jim, and Julia never forgot what had caused her father to lose faith. Consequently, she would never deny her family. My mother definitely looked like she was a White woman. Because of what happened to her family, Frank, I know she would be visibly upset if you even implied she was anything but African-American. She would correct anyone making that mistake, whether it was a Black woman, who she met at a church picnic, or if she was under the lynching rope of the grand wizard of the KKK.

"My mother, your grandmother, Frank, was a very proud woman," Mattie added and then concluded her story.

"All of the children knew this story, Frank, including your father Fred. He could have never thought that his mother was anything other than who she was and by all rules we'd ever know, she was a strong and proud Black woman."

# CHAPTER 12

## The Confrontation

When Frank's flight departed Fresno the following day, he jokingly thought he was happy to be clearing out of Dodge before sundown. As compelling as much of the evidence was, Frank was still unconvinced that there was any definitive connection to this family.

He had decided he was going to talk with his boss, David Brewer, before he came to any conclusions. It was not because David was African-American. He wanted to talk with David because he was about the best friend Frank had in Portland, a friendship apparently mutually shared.

As he reclined the seat and turned off the overhead light, he mussed that the best part of these trips was getting back home. For the rest of the flight, he did not think much more about what he had learned over the last few days in Fresno, as he drifted off to sleep.

Frank loved to fly. Be it as an airline passenger on a "heavy iron" Boeing 777, or tooling along on his own in David Brewer's Cessna 150, the plane that he had first learned to pilot himself, he really did not care.

So as usual, the sound of the commuter airline's twin turboprop engines throttled back was enough to break his light sleep. As a pilot familiar with the Portland airport, Frank knew they were somewhere south of Eugene, starting their descent to intercept the "MOXEE SIX" instrument approach into Portland, about fifteen or twenty minutes until they were on the ground… home sweet home.

*In a few weeks, maybe,* thought Frank as he opened his eyes, *I'll be making these approaches on my own, if I can get past that danged instrument rating exam.*

Once he got his instrument rating, he could use the company's Mooney 20E to fly himself to Fresno and not have to deal with the schedules and such. David would say to him, "If you positively, absolutely have to be there on time, fly United, or get your instrument rating."

Before he knew it, Frank was on the ground in the Portland International Airport terminal, with a smiling Barbara waiting to meet him as he walked from the secured area. "Hi, Barb," said Frank as he kissed his girlfriend.

"How was your trip?"

"Well, I don't think I'll have to go back down until after the first of the year," said Frank. "North Fresno Public Schools seemed to be happy with the quick demonstration I did yesterday morning. I'm working in Salem next week, so I'll be home every day next week. Even better, I'm also here in town the week after. Small blessings, wouldn't you say?"

"And Friday night, we're at Dr. Salinger's retirement dinner. Too bad David is out of town on business." Then Barbara added, "Faye will be there."

Frank laughed and asked, "That's where he said he'd be, huh?" Frank knew that David was going to be at home with his feet kicked up in front of the television tomorrow evening.

Barbara also laughed and in a sarcastic manner said, "You're such a good boyfriend, Frank. You're going to the dinner with your honey," and then wickedly added, "whether you want to or not!"

Not having any checked baggage, the two continued walking out the airport to Barbara's car.

"Well, Frank," asked Barbara as she started the car, "where are we headed? Your house or mine?"

Frank thought for several seconds and answered, "As much as I'd rather spend the rest of this evening with you, Barb, I have some things I need to prepare for work tomorrow morning. Better drop me at my house and I'll pick you up tomorrow evening to go to the retirement dinner party."

The conversation shifted to Barbara catching Frank up on some things that had occurred with a mutual friend over the few days Frank was away on business. Although it appeared Frank was paying close attention, Frank in fact could not help internally reflecting upon the information he learned in Fresno.

Thus, Frank nearly ran into his house as soon as Barbara dropped him off, going straight into his office to see if he could find any information about the

Tedder v. Tedder court case by searching the Internet. This is when Frank first began his research into the Tedder family. Funny thing about research, every answer tends to create more questions, Frank would have no idea that each question and answer would pull him into this same office repeatedly during the next couple of years.

The next morning was a Friday, and generally following a return from a site trip, Frank typically would soon be on his way to enjoying his weekend by noontime. However, today Frank had decided to sit down with his friend David Brewer for a few minutes before leaving for the weekend. David Brewer was also Frank's boss.

It is important to understand some things about David Brewer. Mainly, David ran a different business operation because David was a quite different kind of individual. He and his older brother and sister were all born and raised in Washington, D.C., by a widowed mother who for most of her adult life worked as a congressional staff assistant for a powerful and senior Member of Congress from Arkansas.

When David entered high school, his mom got her boss to arrange for David to work as a congressional page and attend the exclusive and prestigious high school set-up at the United States Capitol for pages back in those days.

As an African-American, David grew up in a predominantly African-American working-class neighborhood in upper Northwest Washington, D.C., just off Georgia Avenue, a few miles or so north of Howard University. Until he went to work as a page, his friends from his childhood were mostly other African-Americans.

David always had a piece of a memory emanating from when he was maybe four or five, being towed around the Washington Monument grounds with his mother and a man who apparently was his father. What stuck out most from this memory fragment were the reverberating words, like a preacher's voice he heard repeatedly, "... I have a dream today," and then the crowd erupting into applause each time the phrase came through the loudspeakers.

He recalled listening to the radio as a teenager, WOOK-AM playing the Temptation's hit song *Runaway Child*, and James Brown singing, *I'm Black and I'm Proud*. David could remember in clear detail the United States Army troops rolling down Georgia Avenue in a convoy to squelch the riots during the summer of 1968.

What David remembered most as a child was the fun he had with his friends… skipping with his friends across Georgia Avenue at the busy Van Buran Street intersection to get frozen custard on a hot summer day in the District.

The point is that David was raised very African-American. He met his later-to-be wife, Faye, the daughter of a congressional representative from the southwest, while they were both pages at the Capitol. Faye's mother was Japanese-American. They were incredibly good friends, but never really dated because at the time, David felt that Black men should only date Black women. Upon graduation from high school, they went separate ways, and David moved west to attend the University of California in San Diego.

David did not graduate from UC San Diego. After his second year, he more or less got sucked into the radio business and found himself employed full time doing the news at a small R&B radio station in San Diego.

The fact is that David had a lot of intense and varied interests. Unfortunately, for him, pre-law, his field of study, was not one of them. However, one that was intense was his interests of electronics and eventually computer programming that he pursued as a hobby. Over about ten years, he became an excellent programmer, and in fact developed a couple of programs that were used in the broadcast industry in which he was employed.

Those two programs worked so well, that he took those applications with him in the early nineties when he first established Pluto Software in Sunnyvale, California. The business took off. Then, quite by accident, he ran into Faye, who by then was finishing her specialty training at Stanford's Medical school.

They first just picked up as friends, but soon started dating. Less than a year later they were married. When David decided to expand their company, he and Faye moved their business to Portland.

David encouraged disagreement in the office. He wanted all his employees to be passionate about what they did, and to stand up and challenge what they thought was important. He would say to his employees, "If it is not good enough to fight for, it must not be that good."

There were many who thought David allowed an unprofessional workplace. If he heard the two fulltime programmers in a heated discussion about how to do a certain thing, he would just ignore it, along with the slamming doors, if he did not hear things getting too personal.

David believed that is how his company came up with ideas and approaches that were radically different from anyone else in their niche of the software business. You could even override David himself if you could present a convincing argument, and that indeed happened on many occasions.

Frank fit right in. Yes, David would tell you he liked Frank from the day he walked into the conference room, a typical college freshman wearing a shirt and tie, and blue Levi's jeans with tennis shoes. He would tell you that this young man was by now a good close friend, beyond the workplace. He would have not only given Frank the shirt off his back, he would have also offered him his tie and jacket.

At eleven o'clock, Frank knocked a couple of times on David's half-closed door, and then stuck his head through the doorway. Seeing David with his back turned on his computer, Frank said, "David... you ready for me?"

"Yeah, Frank... just give me a second to finish this thought," David replied.

Frank walked over to a small conference table to the left of David's desk, sat down in one of the three chairs, and waited about a minute or so while David finished typing.

David started talking as he got up and then moved to a chair at the conference table. "Okay, Mister Franklin, how was Fresno?"

"I got their system up and runnin' before they ever knew I was comin'," said Frank with a short laugh at his own rhyme.

"Their stuff turned out to be pretty straightforward, David. I got all the settings for their system in and tested before the end of day on Tuesday. You know, we could have done everything from here," said Frank.

"Of course, we could have, Frank, but you know that's not the reason I have you going down there. We are at the start of a severe economic downturn. That attendance intervention program, even though they will not say it, is a moneymaker for those districts, especially in California, where they have already started cutting everything to hell. We get those folks at North Fresno Public singing praises, and we can get all of those districts down there using it, even now."

"Thanks, David. I guess that means I am going to be spending a lot of time in the sunny San Joaquin Valley for the next year or so."

"Yep, you definitely got that right. By the way, did you drive up into Kings Canyon like I was telling you about?"

"Actually, no," Frank said.

"I thought you said you were finished by Tuesday evening?" David continued, "I would have thought you'd have taken off Wednesday afternoon and shot some pictures up there."

"That is kind of why I wanted to talk to you today before you leave for the weekend, David." Frank got up and walked over to the door that he shut. "Something a little on the weird side happened while I was there."

"You mean weird at the jobsite?" David asked, looking concerned.

"No," replied Frank as he sat back down. "Weird meaning, I met some people who were trying to convince me they were my family."

"Okay… I take it this was unexpected?"

"Oh, that's an understatement," replied Frank.

"But I would have thought that was something good," David said back to his friend. "I thought that was something you wanted to happen?"

"Well, I did too," replied Frank. "I was not expecting that to happen out of the blue. And I just really did not consider that my father might be so different. First, if this man is my father, he died a few months ago."

David said, "I'm sorry, Frank. I know you hoped to get a chance to meet him someday."

"I said 'if' he was my father." Frank then added, "You see, the relatives of his that I met are African-American."

David could not help bursting out laughing. He could see that Frank did not see anything funny, and he held up his hands and forced himself to stop laughing. "Okay, I can see how that might be a little weird. So, you thought it would be prudent to consult your only Black friend who just happens to be your boss. Okay… I get it. Tell me the story, Frank," as he sat back to listen to what was sure to be at the very least, an entertaining story.

Frank told David how he met John Assorian the previous Sunday, and explained he was a little shocked when Gayle walked into the restaurant, and how he tried to find anything in what he heard to be untrue.

"That would be a surprise, even to me if that table was turned a bit," said David. "Before you start auditioning for *Soul Train*, I'm curious why you think that the man in the photo he showed you is actually your dad?"

"I don't think he is," Frank responded.

"You mean you don't *think* he is your father, or you don't *want* him to be your father," David immediately asked.

Frank thought a moment before he responded. "Ah… both, I think. But I think the '*don't want to claim him*' part has more to do with him being such a liar."

David reclined back in his chair and said, "Tell me the rest of the story."

Frank spent the next ten or fifteen minutes telling David about the time he spent with Mattie Wednesday afternoon. When Frank was telling him about Fred running away from home in the late thirties, David made the comment, "I think if someone wants to survive, they might do just like this man did in those days."

David said, "I would not be so quick to condemn someone because they choose to survive. Once you go down that course for a while, you can easily become caught up in the lie you created for that survival purpose. I'm not saying it's right, but maybe you need to honestly ask yourself if you would not at least have been tempted to do the same thing?"

"I do have to admit," David added, "… that it took a lot of effort to keep his family separated from his group of white friends so long, especially in a city the size of Fresno. Neither knew anything about the other until he was on his deathbed, huh?"

Frank laughed for the first time during the conversation. "It's really funny. Gayle, Mattie's daughter, said that at the family's Thanksgiving and Christmas dinners she'd host at her home, he would always insist that Gayle make him six sweet potato pies to take with him. David, I've never even tasted sweet potato pie. Anyhow, Gayle said she thought her uncle was just being a pig.

"Well, it turns out that after her Uncle Fred would leave the holiday dinner at Gayle's house, she had no idea that he'd take these six pies to six of his very close White friends that had fallen in love with Gayle's pies some years earlier.

"Gayle said she thought her uncle was just very self-centered because he'd always leave right after the holiday meal without spending much time intermingling with his family. Turns out he was on a schedule. Yeah, he was definitely caught up in his lies."

Frank asked rhetorically, "But you know what really got me?" Then he answered the rhetorical question. "Fred's family has the type of history that anyone would want in their background, regardless of their race." Frank then told David what Mattie had told him about her parents, grandparents, and great-grandparents.

Frank spoke in an excited voice when he told the story about William and Adline Tedder. "Just two or three years out of slavery, and this White man *marries* his former slave. He defies the community, his previous family, and for the next thirty-five years, provides their common children with the best he can offer, and tries in vain to leave them the wealth he accumulated. You could not make up a better story for a Hollywood movie.

"And David, this Adline woman had to be something really special to deal with the same circumstance in the manner she did. Oh, yeah, I'd be proud of them if they were in my family."

That's when David interjected. "Well, Frank, a lot of black families have stories about relationships between some white man during or after slavery, that I think over the years, they get to be told in a manner that makes the relationship a bit more pretty. The reality is probably not that positive. Most of those Black women were forced, or to put it bluntly, raped. It is highly unlikely they were in an open marriage just after the Civil War.

"I also hear you saying that the fact this family has this White lineage somehow makes them okay… is that what you're implying, Frank?"

That last question made Frank think for a minute before he responded, "No, no… you don't understand, David… no, not at all. I just think it is so novel and the people were so courageous. I'd feel the same if you took the race part out of it."

Frank continued, "What did intrigue me is that the information is documented in a way that makes it apparent that a real wrong was done to this family at the turn of the century. You remember a few weeks ago when we were listening to that radio talk show when driving back from Salem?"

"Sure, I do, Frank. I think you agreed that an election of a Black President, or just the real possibility of Obama being elected indicates that racism is behind us… yeah, I remember that. Right before I changed the station. What's your point, Frank?"

Frank replied in a musing manner, "I think there might be a little more to all this race junk. I always thought that most of this stuff was based on stories, and were mostly just that, stories. I just never imagined that these horror stories were factually verifiable and real… they actually happened.

"When I got home yesterday evening, I spent about four or five hours on-line and found the two court cases that they told me about. It is all there in detail, exactly as Mattie and Gayle tell the story. When I look up the census records, I am sure that too is going to fit exactly with the story. It would not surprise me if I am able to eventually dig out the marriage certificate."

David started to respond, but Frank held up his hand to indicate there is more. "And to take it a step further, the Supreme Court in South Carolina takes the property the Black children inherited and gives it to the White children, fifteen years after the old guy dies. And most of his Black children and their children's children still manage to have successful and productive lives. You can't make this stuff up."

"I have to admit, Frank, that is quite different. The fact that there is a ver-ifiable story, all the way into slavery in my experience is unusual," replied David. "I can see how that story would impress you so much. It impresses me."

David went on. "You know what, Frank? It sounds like there is a lot of ev-idence to support the idea that this Fred Burton is your father. My guess is what really got you thinking is that for the first time, you're realizing how much you enjoy being a White man."

David had to struggle to control himself, but still laughed. "And for the first time, you are thinking that it does make a difference, even now in 2008, two days after the election of the first non-white man as the President of this country. I'll bet your neat analysis regarding Barack Obama is a little different than it was last week?"

Frank let out another short laugh, and said, "Okay, David. You're right. I have spent a few minutes pondering why I am so tough on Barack Obama. And you are also right about the part about considering what it would mean to me if I were not White. I am wondering if it will make a difference."

"But Frank," said David, "the reality is that before you get too involved into this deep soul searching, you need to determine if Fred is really your dad. What's your mom say?"

"I don't know. I have not talked to her since last week, and not about this," said Frank.

David replied, "Okay. You might want to do that first. But say she confirms that Fred is your father? There is no law that says you must tell anyone. I promise that unless you go out and announce to the world everything about your newfound family tree, it will make zero difference in the way people relate to you, Frank. You'll still be Frank."

Frank asked, "Well, what about what John Assorian says about children being born with black features?"

David started laughing. "Frank, I think the odds of that happening are ridiculously small. Yeah, you hear a story every now and then. I think that they are mostly stories… urban legends. The fact is, your kids are probably going to look like either you or their mother, probably a little of both. If you have a daughter that turns out to have slightly larger lips, well, she won't have to get Botox treatments if she becomes a movie actress."

Even Frank had to laugh at the last comment.

David kept talking. "And Big Brother has not yet got us to the point when we get a routine DNA test to determine our ancestry. We'll probably get some privacy laws in place before that starts happening, although the science is obviously there."

"But what if I want people to know?" asked Frank.

David responded, "That's a different story, one that you'll have to figure out." David started to get up out of his chair, and asked, "You were about to leave when we were finished, right?"

Frank said, "Yep, I was going to head home and take a nap before I get ready for that party tonight. You know the one that you managed to avoid?"

"Tell you what, why don't we go get a five-hundred-dollar cheeseburger," David asked as he got up and walked back toward a closet to retrieve his coat, briefcase, and another bag.

Frank replied, "Do bears play in the forest?"

David laughed. "They most certainly do, unless they're playing in the zoo. Let's rock and roll then."

Frank said, "Absolutely," and nearly ran back to his office to gather his things.

He caught up with David as he was walking out the door, "Liz, call over and make arrangements for Frank and me to go out for a cheeseburger in Six Eight Quebec. We're both out of here for the weekend."

"Okay, David," replied his assistant, who knew exactly what he meant. "I'll tell them about thirty minutes. Have a good weekend, boss."

Thirty minutes later, David and Frank were parking David's 2005 Subaru Outback in a parking space at the Portland-Hillsboro airport. David and Faye lived a modest lifestyle for their careers and status. They lived in a small home, in a modest neighborhood of Portland, and David drove a three-year-old compact all-wheel drive wagon because he said it was practical for the kinds of activities he pursued.

However, they both had their own pet extravagances. Faye was a little less practical when it came to cars. She splurged every couple of years, this time she had a high-end Mercedes convertible, just a few months old. However, Faye's splurges were nothing when compared to David's extravagances.

David was a general aviation pilot and loved airplanes. He owned three of them. The first was a forty-year-old Cessna 150, a little two-seat high-winged single-engine airplane he personally bought just after he learned to fly in San Diego. The second airplane he owned was what he called his first *real* airplane, a thirty-year-old four-seat, low-winged, and relatively fast single-engine Mooney 20E. He bought that airplane for the company after the business took off in Sunnyvale.

People who are not into flying are sometimes shocked to hear the age of most of the small planes they see buzzing around in the sky. They are still expensive, and David spent much more to keep them in top-notch shape.

However, the Big Plane as he called it was Six Eight Quebec, the reference to the tail number of N1168Q, a near brand-new Socata TBM 750. It was a propeller-driven single-engine turbine that was loaded with just about everything a pilot or passenger could think of or imagine and cost well more than a million dollars when he purchased it for the company two years earlier. It was also fast.

David's other "hobby" was giving flight instruction, not for the money, but because he liked to do it. One inner-city kid who he met while the youngster was in high school and subsequently instructed was about to graduate from the aviation-oriented Emery-Riddle University and figured to soon be a commercial airline pilot. David taught Frank to fly and was now working with him to get his instrument rating.

He was also giving Frank the opportunity to build time in the Big Airplane so he could qualify with the insurance company to fly it himself. Matter of fact, David was going to send him to "Flight Safety International" sometime in the next year, after Frank passed his instrument rating exam, to get the final type rating and insurance company required training for the TBM.

So when Frank heard David say, "Let's go get a five-hundred-dollar cheeseburger," he knew he meant they were going to take the Big Airplane out for an hour or so, and that would cost about five hundred dollars in fuel and other operational costs. More importantly, he would get to fly it and log the time as Pilot in Command. The cheeseburger was an option if they landed and had lunch.

Upon arrival at the airport, Frank went right over to the Big Airplane and started the pre-flight walk around and checklist. Liz, David's assistant, had called ahead, so the FBO (Fixed Base Operator) already had the airplane out of the hanger and brought it up in front of the FBO's building. David went inside and pulled the latest weather. A weather front was presently moving out of most of western Oregon, but there was still scattered rain up and down the Willamette Valley, and snow showers in the higher elevations, especially on the eastern side of the Cascades.

When David got into the plane, Frank, already seated in the left seat as the pilot in command, completed the pre-flight checklist. David said to him, "We're above VFR (visual flying rules) minimums right now, let's just go VFR and head down toward Medford."

The airplane was indeed fast. A little more than ten minutes after takeoff and they were already at 11,500 feet over Salem, looking down on beautiful puffs of clouds pock marking the lush green Oregon landscape, two miles below.

"You fly the plane, and I'll talk," Frank heard David saying inside his headset. "You are right about the way people deal with you could be different, Frank. Did I tell you what happened to me a few months ago when I was over in Utah?"

"Okay, I've got the plane," said Frank, then answered David's question. "No. I don't think so," said Frank.

"Well, I was at some airport over in someplace like Bum Town, Utah. The district superintendent had dropped me off at the airport when we finished our meeting earlier. So the sun's going down while I am pre-flighting this airplane while there is still some daylight, and I see this sheriff's car coming toward me from way down the road, like a bat out of hell, kicking up big clouds of dust and all."

About that time, David's narrative was interrupted when the headset crackled, "Socata Six Eight Quebec, you have traffic at ten o'clock, a twin Cessna at three miles westbound, descending out of twelve thousand, five hundred."

"Roger Center, six eight Quebec is looking," Frank replied. Then about five seconds later, David pointed out the window as he clicked the transmit button, "… and we see the traffic now at eleven o'clock, Six Eight Quebec." Frank waited a few seconds, and then turned the big airplane to his left a bit and the other aircraft went buzzing by, well above and far off to his right. It was not remarkably close, but he was on it much faster than he anticipated.

David said, "Okay, Frank. This is a much faster airplane than the Mooney, and you will be on top of something before you even know it. Don't hesitate to alter your course behind the traffic if you need to but do it early. You have to adjust your brain to think faster in this airplane."

After about a minute of silence, David went back to his story. "So this sheriff walks up with his hand on the butt of his revolver, and starts asking me for my ID, and what I was doing out here at the airport. He didn't believe me when I told him it was my airplane.

"Honestly, I was a little scared, it's getting dark, and this country cop is grilling me. I mean, I am showing him my name painted on the side of the airplane, the airplane registration with my name as the owner, my pilot's license, my driver's license, even my passport that I keep in my flight bag.

"He still didn't believe me. I had to wait until the superintendent that had dropped me off earlier finally got to a place where his cellphone worked, almost 45 minutes later. He was going to arrest me, if the superintendent did not verify who I was."

Frank asked, "So you were pissed?"

"Ah… I'll get back to you after I think about it some… Yes, I was pissed to say the least." David thought a moment before continuing. "But not really surprised. That kind of thing has been happening to me and my friends for as far back as I can remember. But here's the thing for you, Frank, you won't have to deal with that unless you choose. You obviously don't look like a Black man, Frank."

Frank commented, "That's just like Fred did. So, you think it's okay to lie?"

David responded, "That's my point. If that sheriff's officer said, 'Tell me you're White, and I won't hassle you,' guess what I would have said to that cop, out in the middle of nowhere at night?

"Look, Frank, you've been around me with that old ninety going on 109-year-old geezer that I occasionally take flying. You know, old man Sampson was a Tuskegee Airman during World War Two. And you've gone golfing with me and those two clowns from my church that seem to like hanging with you for some strange reason."

"That's because I'm a much better golfer than you," replied Frank with a laugh.

"Seriously, you know that I am a very black man, beyond my appearance. I don't have to say it, I live it proudly. But you also don't see me plastering my picture all over our company's materials, do you? Am I being dishonest? I don't think so. But why should I provide any more information beyond what anyone needs to make a decision for doing business with my company?" David rhetorically asked.

"What I am saying is that I am a Black man, but that's nowhere near all of me. I am David Brewer, who is much, much more than that. Regardless of what you choose or do not choose to make known about yourself, Frank, you will always still be Frank Malloy, period. That can never be a lie," David concluded, but then had to add something else.

"If the folks at the Portland NAACP could hear me talking now, they might drop my membership," and then he laughed.

Neither spoke for the next few minutes until Frank asked, "What do we do when we get to Medford? We're almost there. You want to land there and get something to eat?"

"I can see that. No," answered a thinking David. "Why don't you put us into the system as an IFR popup, and head over for the non-precision VOR approach into Bend? I'll get the approach plates for you."

Frank replied, "Oh, I see what you're trying to do. You want to get me to Bend to visit my mom."

Sounding a little exasperated while he fumbled through his tablet computer to find the Bend approach instructions, David kept talking. "No, you are going to be taking the instrument check ride in a few weeks and I know who is going to administer that exam. It won't hurt you to get some experience in actual instrument conditions.

"Trust me, Frank. She is not going to let you fly a cushy, undemanding precision approach at Hillsboro and hand you an instrument rating certificate. She's going to take you to one of these mountain airports and have you hand-fly a difficult VOR approach, in weather if possible, among other things I would imagine. You can visit your mom if you want… that's up to you. Might not be a bad idea, though. Here's the approach plate," and he handed the tablet to Frank.

Frank complied and got on the radio to get an IFR clearance and vectors to where the approach would start. What David said was true. A non-precision approach is, by definition, about the most dangerous kind of approach for landing you can execute when the weather was bad, because it was not precise.

However, in many cases, and especially at small uncontrolled airports, that kind of approach is all you have. It meant you flew to a VOR (Very high-frequency Omni-directional Radio) beacon that had directional radio spokes for each compass ordinal where you would start the procedure.

You crossed the beacon at a specific altitude, and then turned to ride a specific "spoke" of the VOR at a specific speed, in one or more steps, each step for a specific amount of time. During each time interval step, you stayed at or above a specified minimum safe altitude, until you had stepped down to the last minimum safe altitude. You flew that last step for a specific amount of time at precisely that minimum altitude.

If you saw the airfield and the surrounding environment before the time expired, and you could safely land, you proceeded to land, flying the remaining approach while keeping the field and everything else in visual sight. Otherwise, you flew a missed approach heading back to a designated safe altitude. If you did everything right, that was great. If not, well you could end up having an awfully bad day, possibly becoming a scorch mark on the side of a mountain.

In this airplane, the state-of-the-art avionics could fly the entire approach on its own, right down to the final decision point. But Frank was trying to get experience in flying the procedure manually in preparation for his instrument rating exam.

Frank flew a perfect approach mostly blind in light snow all the way down to nearly the last minimum safe altitude where they broke out the overcast, with the airfield right in front of the windshield. After they were on the ground, David asked Frank to pull up in front of the airport terminal building, but before he could shut down the engine, David started talking to Frank.

"Frank. I lied. Tell your mother I said hello. I'll come back and get you tomorrow afternoon in the Mooney." David added, "By the way, you flew a perfect approach. You're going to ace that check ride."

"But David, I have all but sworn to Barbara I'd be at that party this evening. I mean, I can't…"

David cut Frank off, shaking his head, "I've known Barbara for much longer than you, Frank. When you talk to Barbara, you tell her I made you go visit your mom. It will be fine. I am going to take her to that thing tonight myself. The sacrifices I make. You owe me one, Frank."

Frank got out of the airplane, shut the air-stair door, and walked to a place where David could see he was clear, and then waved goodbye. David brought up the throttles and taxied back out to the departure runway and took off without any delay.

On the ground, it was raining lightly, and it was just a little after two in the afternoon. The Bend airport was several miles to the northeast of the city of Bend, Oregon. However, this was home for Frank, even though he had not lived here for nearly fifteen years.

One of his friends from high school who ran one of the aircraft engine repair service businesses agreed to give Frank a quick ride to where his mom worked on the northern end of town. This was not the first time Frank had popped into town in this manner.

When he walked into his mother's office, she looked up from her work, surprised to see Frank. "Frank, what you are doing here? Is David with you?" she asked as she got up from her desk, walked over, and gave him a big hug and kiss on the cheek. At 59, Frank's mom was still an attractive woman.

"No. David dropped me off a few minutes ago, Mom. He told me to say hello for him. I thought I'd spend the evening with you if you don't mind," asked Frank.

"Of course, you can. You don't get home enough. Why don't you take my car and go over to the store and pick us up a couple of steaks that I can make for dinner? I don't think there is much at the house to make for dinner. Are you going to stay until Sunday?"

"No. I am going to head back sometime tomorrow. But yeah, Mom, the steaks sound like a good idea for tonight. I'll come back and get you at 3:30 when you get off," said Frank.

By six-thirty, Frank and his mom were finishing dinner. That's when Cheryl commented, "You are being a little quiet. Why don't you tell me what's on your mind, Franklin?" She knew her son.

"Okay." Frank took a moment to gather his thoughts and said, "I found Fred." He said it as a simple fact.

Cheryl was a little stunned by that news. "What do you mean you found Fred? I assume you are talking about your father?"

"Yes, Mom, but he actually died several months ago. He was living in Fresno," Frank stated. "I met his sister and his niece."

"Fred died? That is not something I was prepared to hear. More than thirty years later, and I still thought I'd somehow talk with him again," Cheryl said as her eyes filled with a few tears. There was a bigger thought going through her mind that Frank probably now knew everything.

"Mom, why didn't you just tell me that Fred was African-American?" Frank asked. Frank was not angry. He had got past most of that over the last few days.

Frank was surprised when she answered because she just seemed to accept the inevitable. She said, "Franklin, I did not want you to go through what you are no doubt going through right now. I can hear that this has been weighing on you. Do you remember just after you graduated from high school and I told you about my previous life and about Fred?"

"Yes, I do," replied Frank.

"Well, I started to tell you about Fred's family, but the truth is that I was not proud of the decision I made," explained Cheryl.

"I told you at that time, I was trying to protect you. The truth is I was mostly trying to protect myself. I was afraid of what people would think of me. I thought I'd have a tough time living and working at that hillbilly motel in Sacramento if Sally and her family knew about Fred. I certainly didn't want anyone around this metropolis to know about Fred.

"The funny thing is that what I told you about my life in Portland when I was in my late teens and twenties was much worse than being associated with Fred. Yet I told you all about that.

"That last night I was with Freddy, he told me about when he first ran away from home, and what he saw happening to some Black people who were living as hobos. The things that happened to him when he was a child out on his own were horrible. You know, a man almost killed him when he physically threw Fred off a freight train in Oklahoma, he said because he was Black. And another man he worked for beat him up and left him for dead out in the desert for the same reason, at least so he believed."

Cheryl got up and kissed her son on the forehead, and started to clear the table, and continued talking to Frank. "But all during that last conversation, Franklin, the only thing I could think of was that he had dragged me and my emotions into this with a lie. I was worried about what Mama would say. How my daddy would have reacted if he were alive. And to top it off, I was very much in love with him." She stopped what she was doing and looked directly at her son. "Go figure that one out, Franklin."

Cheryl came back to the table, sat back down across from Frank, and then continued, "Here he is trying to come clean with me. I am judging him as a liar. Yet, he thinks my name is Margaret. I never even told him my name. I didn't even consider what he would have thought of me, if he would even want to be involved with me if he knew about my past... what I did with those men when I lived in Portland. Yet I said he was the liar. You tell me who the liar is?"

"Well, Mom," Frank interrupted, "Fred lied to everyone. His own family only found out when he was dying that he was living two separate lives, for years. He had a group of White friends, I mean close friends that had no idea of his family. They thought he was a White man."

"Consider this, Franklin," she said. "He told me just about everything about himself, and I got up and ran out of his life because I did not like what I heard. He was every bit as tied up with me emotionally as I thought I was with him. You think that his experience with me might have determined what he told other people down the road? I pretty much confirmed the worst consequences in his mind, I think.

"Ironically, after I was back at your Grandma's house a few weeks later, I realized the hypocrisy of my actions with Freddy. So, I thought I'd go back to California and try to find him in a month or so. But a few weeks later, I found out I was pregnant with you, and that just added more confusion to my thinking," she said.

"So, over the next seven or eight months, I pondered how I was going to deal with this subject with you. I told Mom that Freddy had done something really bad, so bad that I could not talk about it." Cheryl laughed. "Mama thought Fred had killed someone and wanted to call the police. That's when I came up with the name Fred Langton, and that's the name I wrote on the birth certificate. Until she died, I never even hinted that your father was Black.

"What else is funny when I think about it now, Franklin, Mama would have been happier just to know I had got out of that bad life I was previously involved in. She may not have liked the idea of Fred initially, but I think she would have accepted Fred just fine in the long run. I underestimated your grandma, but I was a scared and confused young woman.

"You know, about five or six years ago, a man who was running trucks up from Fresno came into my office to inquire about his drivers refueling here. He knew Fred. Told me Fred had stopped driving because of that bad knee he injured when he was in the Army. Never saw the man again. But I guess I really could have found Fred if I wanted.

"I just got so caught up in this whole thing over the years. I could never bring myself to tell you, Franklin. I hope you can forgive me. In the long run, it really did become all about you. I did not want you to go through what must be hard for you at the moment." Then she added, "I really love you, Franklin. I thought it would be simpler if you never found out. That was a mistake."

"I know that, Mom," answered Frank. "Earlier this week, I might have been a little more upset. But I have come to understand, at least a little, that none of this information changes who I am."

Frank got up and started to load the dishwasher for his mom. "Was his full name Fred Langston Burton?"

She took her son's hand and squeezed it. "Yes, it was. This is your father."

Frank turned, hugged his mom, and replied, "That's what I thought you'd say. You know what? I am not going to think about this anymore tonight. Would you mind if I take your car and go out for an hour or so?"

"Of course, you can. I am in for the night, Frank." His mom thought a moment and said, "But if you are going to the bowling alley, don't have more than a couple of beers, Frank. They have got real nasty about stopping people for drinking and driving around town recently."

Frank went to his old room and changed into a pair of jeans that still fit and headed out for the local bowling alley. Cheryl did not need to remind him about drinking. He was the two-drink kid on the few occasions he would visit any kind of place that featured alcohol. Mainly, he liked stopping off at the local bowling alley when in town because that is where he would find some of his old friends.

As it turned out, going down to the bowling alley to lighten things up appeared to be just the right thing to do. As soon as he walked into the small bar and lounge, he saw one of his best friends from high school, Sara Jane, seated alone at a table in the lounge, having some fries while her husband was out bowling with his league team.

They had been sitting and laughing at the stories that Frank was telling about his new girlfriend in Portland, and some of the funny things Sara's kids had done. The evening was perfect up until Ben Reynolds walked up to their table.

"Brother Franklin, what's going on?" Ben spoke in a slightly slurred voice. Ben was already about a quarter 'til drunk. He looked at Sara and said, "How ya doing, Sara?"

Frank jumped up smiling, happy to see his old friend who he hugged while he shook his hand and said, "I see you decided to grow some hair, buddy."

"Well, you know, Frank, I had to grow up and get a job," Ben replied and started laughing.

Frank noticed that Sara had become quiet and was looking away from Ben. It was obvious that she did not want to have a discussion with Ben. Before Frank could say anything, Ben said, "I gotta hit the head. You and Sara wait right here. I wanna catch up on old times."

After Ben headed for the bathroom and had gotten far enough away, Sara looked at Frank and said, "I can't stand that piece of worthless crap! I will not be here when he gets back Frank." She started to quickly gather up her things in preparation to leave.

Frank grabbed her arm and said, "Slow down. I'll tell you when he's coming back from the bathroom. It's all the way on the other side of the alley. I'm looking right at him and he hasn't even got there yet. What's up with you and Ben?"

"You know he just got out of prison less than a year ago, right?" Sara asked.

"Yeah, sure, I know all about that," said Frank. Ben had indeed spent five years in prison, convicted of manufacturing crystal methamphetamine with two of his older friends.

"Mom told me when she heard he was back in town last year," Frank added.

"Did you see the way he looks, Frank?"

"Well, he looks better than the last time I saw him. It looks like he got out of that skinhead crap he was into in high school," Frank replied.

"Are you kidding me, Frank?" Sara said, nearly yelling. In a lower voice she continued, "Going to prison was like going to University of Nazi for Ben.

The only reason he let his hair grow back was to cover those Nazi tats all over his head. No one would hire him the way he looked.

"He's got a tattoo on the back of his head that says *White Power* and swastikas on both sides of his head. If he took his shirt off, you'd call the police, Frank. He has racist prison tattoos all over his body. You can see the top of a swastika right above the top of his shirt collar."

Frank simply said, "Yeah, Sara, but he's still Ben. You remember, our friend, the one who took the blame when we nearly got busted for smoking marijuana at school?"

"That was more than ten or fifteen years ago, Frank," she said. "Ben has got much further out there. I don't want anyone like that around me and my kids. Ronald, his best friend when we were kids, avoids him too.

"He was on the news a few months back, protesting with Nazi flags in front of City Hall for hiring that African-American-owned paving company out of Portland. That paving company is the only reason why Ronald is working right now.

"Yeah, Frank, Ben and that group of trashy skinheads caused a big stink. That company got that job because they were the lowest bidder, and they have done a lot of good work for the city. And they always hire local people from here, like my husband. They'd probably even hire him and his friends if they didn't act like a bunch of bigoted asses and could figure out how to spell their own names."

Sara got up from her seat and leaned over the table as she spoke. "He is a racist, Frank. I do think he has some other serious problems, but I do not intend to be sucked into trying to fix someone who does not want to be fixed. Tell him my husband came and got me. I don't care, tell him whatever you want."

She started walking away so fast that Frank had to raise his voice to say goodbye.

A few minutes later Ben walked back to the table and sat down as Frank looked at him with a grin.

"Time to start refilling after that deposit," said Ben. "Where did Sara go?"

"Ronald came and got her. She said to tell you goodbye," Frank answered.

"Sara is not the same as I remember her, Frank," Ben responded. "You know, I was in the Joint for a while. It was not that bad."

Frank chose his next words somewhat carefully. "Maybe she thinks you have changed a little, Ben. I can see that you are sporting a few more tats. If I didn't know you, those tattoos would be a little scary to me."

Ben smiled broadly and said, "You and Sara have no reason to be afraid of me. I have these tats to let people know I am there for them. I am there for you and Sara. We've got a lot of history, Frank. I am there for the White race."

Ben glanced around the bar, and then pulled a small semi-automatic handgun from his jacket pocket that he displayed to Frank in a way that no one else could see.

Frank, looking very alarmed, asked, "What the hell are you doing with that? You want to shoot someone? You can go back to prison if they catch you with that, you know."

"Naw, Frank," Ben answered. "I don't shoot people. I just use this for poppin' cans."

Frank relaxed a bit and asked, "Just cans, huh?"

"Yeah, *Africans, Mexicans, Puerto Ricans*," and then started laughing in a very scary and hysterical way.

He abruptly stopped laughing and added, "They ain't people, Frank. Maybe mud people, zogs, spicks, and grease heads. The Lord doesn't care if we clear out all that garbage. This country was made for people like me and you, Frank. White people!"

Of course, considering all that had happened to Frank over the last week, he thought for a moment and smiled. "How do you become a member of this club you're in, Ben?"

Ben smiled excitedly and answered, "You just have to be White and willing to stand up for White people. You want to join, Frank? A stand-up guy like you, Frank, would be a major asset for the movement. We've got a few other stand-up guys like you, Frank, right here in town."

Frank leaned back in his chair and shook his head with a look of disbelief. "Are you kidding me? I don't believe in that crap you're into. Never have. Tell me, Ben, how do you and your friends know your new members are even White people? You guys require a blood test or something? Piss in a cup… what?"

Frank looked serious and leaned forward. "You know, you don't exactly have blue eyes and blond hair, Ben. Are you even sure you're one hundred percent White?"

Ben started laughing. "Frank, you can look at me and see that I'm White. I can spot a nigger or a Jew at fifty feet. They teach us how to recognize niggers and Jews."

"You think so? Okay," said Frank again, shaking his head, looking astonished by his friend's statement.

Ben posed a question to Frank. "By the way, do you still work for that affirmative action nigger and his Jap nip-bitch wife? I bet that you and a bunch of smart White men do all the real work and come up with all the ideas. He takes all the credit and keeps all the money, doesn't he?"

Frank coolly responded, "Mister Brewer actually pays all of us rather well. He's also about the most creative programmer I have ever heard of Ben. I'd say that he's probably written more computer code than me and the rest of the staff combined have ever written. You and your new buddies need to wake up and see how the world really works."

"Hey, Frank, I got an idea." Ben started laughing. "Why don't I get some of my White brothers to come up to Portland and kidnap that Jap bitch and make the nigger pay to get her back?"

Frank seemed to ignore the comment and just got up. "You're drunk, Ben. And I told Mom I'd have her car back home by now." Frank walked around to Ben and extended his hand.

Ben got up to shake Frank's hand. "You're my buddy, Frank."

"You too, Ben. You know I love you like a brother. We've got a lot of history like you said."

Frank pulled Ben as if to hug him, but instead grabbed Ben's jacket pocket that held the gun. In a low but deadly serious voice, Frank said, "But if you ever have anything to do with a threat to any of my friends, or anyone for that matter, I will shove this little '*can*' gun up your skinny white ass. I will kick your ass the same way I did when we were kids. You got that?"

He grabbed him tighter. "And I'll be the first one to stand up and make sure they take your White racist butt right back to the joint. Understand?" Then he shoved him away.

Without another word, Frank very nonchalantly walked away leaving Ben looking dumbfounded with his old friend's reaction. Frank drove back to his mother's house.

A lot had transpired over the last week Frank thought as he lay in the bed in which he grew up sleeping. Ben was right. They did share a lot of history.

Sara was right in that Ben had taken some bad turns and appeared to be on an even worse road. However, Frank had a greater sense of loyalty than Sara did when it came down to friendships.

He had known Ben from as far back as he could remember. He did not think Ben was a bad person. He just thought of Ben's thinking as very mixed up. In Frank's mind, Ben was still his friend, good and bad together. He would still go to bat for him if it came to it.

The funny thing is that if he and Ben had this conversation a week earlier, Frank would not have got sucked into Ben's racist-toned talk in the way he did this evening. Even though he never agreed with any of Ben's junk, he would have laughed it off a week ago. The fact is that his perspective had changed, just as he and David had talked about earlier that day.

The next morning, he took his mom out for a late breakfast. Then as promised, David and Faye picked him up at the Bend airport in the early afternoon. The Mooney was a much smaller airplane, only comfortable for two. Therefore, Frank squeezed into the back and let Faye have some comfort on the 45-minute ride back to Portland.

The weather was perfect. At 6,500 feet, he could clearly see Mount Hood, eighty miles to the north. Oregon was between the weather system that exited last night, and another that would push into the area later that evening. David and Frank talked incessantly over the headset intercom, and after about ten minutes into the trip, Faye said, "I am going to let the two of you talk about flying."

Then she unplugged the airplane's headset, pulled out a paperback book and her personal headphones to listen to some music on her cellphone. She connected the phone and settled in, reading and listening to music for the rest of the trip.

Frank could not wait to change the subject. After Faye had unplugged, Frank spoke into his headset. "You were right, David."

"You mean about talking to your mom?"

"Well, that too." Frank was staring out the window thinking. "Really, I thought about everything. I think at this point I am going to give this whole subject some space."

"Good for you, Frank. You woke up this morning and found out you were still the same Frank?"

"Yes, I did. And I figured out that there is more to consider before I start spilling my guts to everyone. Like you said, this really is private and for now, it is on a need-to-know basis. For now, you and maybe Faye are the only people who need to know."

David spoke again. "That's your business, Frank. The conversations we have had are between the two of us. I don't have to tell you that you can talk to me anytime about this stuff."

Then David made a hard-left banked turn to head over and cross the mountains into the Willamette Valley and home.

# CHAPTER 13

## I Am Who I Am

One might want the happy conclusion to this story to occur right here. Frank accepts who he is but decides to keep it to himself for the rest of his life and lives happily ever after. The problem is that is not what happened.

What really happened was much more complex. Fate had come along and had reshuffled the deck of cards that represented Frank's life, and now dealt him a handful of jokers. The first joker to appear was more than a year later when the subject resurfaced from an unexpected trigger.

About that time, Frank found himself having dinner at a downtown Portland restaurant with his girlfriend Barbara, and David and Faye Brewer. David was talking about an idea he had for a new program in a general, but excited way. He liked to bounce new ideas off both Frank and Faye.

As they were eating, David explained, "This reporting program is a big departure from the forms-based systems we have deployed out in the school districts. It will be able to run through a service from the forms system, or we can sell it as a standalone cloud service over the World Wide Web with a high encryption level so the schools will not be afraid of it. I got the basic system coded, Frank."

Frank was eating a delicious stuffed seafood dish as David was talking. He was feeling a little flushed and thought to himself that it might not be a good idea to eat any more of his meal.

However, he was also fascinated with David's idea and commented, "You know, David, I can see how that little addition gets us enough truly unique features that we can start thinking about moving on to a full Student Information System. Use some of your insurgency strategy and surprise the competition."

"Oh...," David sarcastically said, "why didn't I think of that?"

"I don't know. Maybe great minds think alike," said a laughing Frank. As he made the last comment, he had to force himself to swallow hard before he took his next breath.

Barbara commented, "Can't you two talk about anything besides computer programs and flying. It's Saturday night. Give it a rest."

Faye was laughing and saying, "I just hope he's done tinkering with it. Maybe I can finally get some sleep. Turn it over to the other programmers, David. That man has been sitting in that little office next to the bedroom every night for the last three or four months until three and four in the morning, whooping and hollering every time something works. He's like a little kid with a new toy when he gets to coding an idea."

Everyone was laughing with Faye, except for Frank, who had become noticeably quiet. Faye looked at Frank, and as an anesthesiologist who is familiar with the symptoms of anaphylactic shock, knew immediately what was happening.

She said, "Frank, are you alright?" However, Faye already knew the answer to that question. His lips had taken on a blue tint, indicating that he was not getting enough oxygen.

Faye spoke as a command to her husband, "Get him on the floor on his back!" David was already catching Frank as he started to fall out of his chair and was struggling a bit when a man seated at the adjacent table seeing and hearing what was happening, got up and helped David get Frank lying down on his back.

Barbara was a surgical nurse who worked with Faye. No one had to tell Barbara what to do. Although she was crying, she picked up her cellphone, dialed 9-1-1, and requested paramedics and an ambulance.

"David, do you have your pocketknife? I need it or something else sharp," and started loosening Frank's shirt collar. Faye tried to open his month and his tongue had swollen to the point that she could barely force a finger between it and the roof of his mouth. She had to open another airway so Frank could breathe.

Between sobs, Barbara said, "He still has a pulse, but weak. Hang on, Frank... you're going to be alright."

"Barbara, I need a ballpoint pen... see if you can find some hard liquor to sterilize it." Barbara knew exactly what Faye was going to do. She ran over to the bar and snatched the bartender's pen from his chest. "Give me that full bottle of vodka," she said, pointing at the shelf.

While Barbara was getting the pen and liquor, Faye opened the blade of David's pocketknife. She had to get up and walk a couple of steps to a serving table that was set up next to their table. She held it over the flame on a food warmer for a few seconds and went back over to Frank. Barbara had already taken the pen apart and was pouring the vodka all over and through the pen barrel that she handed to Faye, who was again kneeled next to Frank.

Faye took the bottle of vodka, pouring it all over her hands and Frank's neck. She said to Frank, "This is going to hurt. Try not to move or yell."

She looked at Barbara, who was tightly holding Franks head down, and nodded. In one quick motion, she expertly made a puncture at the base of Frank's throat and inserted the pen barrel.

Immediately, Frank's chest started to go up and down normally, and within a few seconds, normal color started to return to his face and lips. Faye put her ear to Frank's chest near his heart and then turned and looked at her husband. "He is not going to expire, and he never went into cardiac arrest. I think he will be okay."

Then she said to Frank, "Relax as much as you can. You're going to be alright, Frank, I promise."

About that time, paramedics arrived, and recognizing Faye as a doctor from the hospital they routinely serviced, deferred the primary treatment to her. She quickly gave Frank an antihistamine injection to alleviate the allergic reaction, and a shot of epinephrine to prevent cardiac arrest. Then she gave Frank a local anesthetic at the neck wound, replaced the pen barrel with a normal trachea tube from the paramedic's kit, and left with the paramedics as they transported Frank to the hospital.

David and Barbara stood together in the restaurant amid a room full of wide-eyed stunned-looking people who were either standing, or sitting at their tables, trying to understand what had just happened.

As Barbara gathered their things amiss the mess they had created, David turning slowly, announced, "My friend had an allergic reaction. My wife, the doctor who treated Frank, says he is going to be okay. I am sorry to mess up your evening."

The room started clapping. David turned to the owner and in a lower voice said, "Send me a bill for all these people in the morning. If anyone wants to come back because their dinner was ruined, make arrangements and I'll pay for that too."

He handed him his card, and he and Barbara left and went directly to the Portland downtown hospital.

Frank received a sedative after he arrived at the emergency room and did not wake up until the next morning.

About mid-morning, Faye came in dressed in surgical greens. "You gave everyone quite a scare last night, Frank. You are not going to be able to talk until they remove that trachea tube later this afternoon. Just nod or shake your head. Barbara was down here when you were sleeping early this morning. She said she's going to be down after she's out of the surgery... she's working now."

Frank nodded.

"Now Frank, I have called your primary physician, Vernon King, and he's going to be here sometime today. Your primary physician is probably going to tell you the same thing I am. That is, you likely had a severe allergic reaction to something you ate that made you go into anaphylactic shock. My guess is that there was some butter used in that stuffed seafood you were eating. Do you understand what I am saying, Frank?"

Again, he nodded.

"Allergies are funny. In your case, eat something with milk, or something that is derived from milk, and maybe you just break out a little, or you get a little stomachache. Or maybe you get away with it, and nothing at all happens. But one day, you have just a tiny amount, and what happened last night, happens. What happened last night can kill you. Bluntly speaking, Frank, if Barbara and I were not there, we would probably all be making plans to attend your funeral today."

Frank nodded.

"Frank. You are going to have to learn how to completely, and I mean completely avoid anything with even the slightest amount of milk. Honestly, Frank, I have only heard of a few documented cases with people who have as severe allergic reactions to milk as you apparently do. It appears to run in families. Is anyone in your family lactose intolerant?"

Frank at first shook his head. Then after he thought about it for a moment longer, stopped and held his hand out palm down, and shook his hand back and forth a few times to indicate he was not sure.

"Well, you think about it, Frank. I would imagine that Dr. King will want to refer you to a specialist." Faye walked over a little closer to Frank and spoke a little less professionally. "You know what, Frank? A doctor I went to medical school with is one of the best in the country dealing with allergies. He is in San Francisco. I'll mention him to Dr. King and see if David can get you on business around the Bay area in the next few weeks."

She took his hand and squeezed it a little and said, "Don't worry, Frank. The worst of this is over. You will be back to your regular self in a week or two. They'll have that trachea tube out later today, but it will take a week or two for you to feel comfortable talking… sorry, but I had to do it, Frank."

Smiling, she added, "It looks like you'll be wearing my scar for the rest of your life." She laughed to lighten things up and added, "I hope Barbara doesn't mind."

Frank was smiling when he nodded his head. He pulled her head down, gave her a kiss on the check, and made his mouth form the word "Thanks," but nothing came out.

Things went just about exactly as Faye had described. The trachea tube was removed, the incision was sewn up later that day, and he went home the next. A week later, he was able to talk and eat without as much pain, but he was going a little crazy lying around at his house.

With a lot of time on his hands, Frank remembered that his apparent father's sister, Mattie, had problems with allergies. A thought went across his mind to give her a call. It took Frank awhile to find Mattie's phone number. Frank was not quite ready to start calling her Aunt Mattie. He had switched phones and had not yet brought all his old telephone listings into his new phone as he wanted to clean out some of the obsolete contacts. He had to open a back-up file on his notebook to retrieve it.

He dialed the number and when she answered, he said, "Hello, Mrs. Meyers?"

She said, "Yes. Who's calling?" His voice was so raspy, that Mattie would not have recognized him if he had called just an hour after he first met her.

"Mrs. Meyers, this is Frank Malloy. I met you and Gayle about a year ago." Then he thought a second and said, "Fred's son." Acknowledging for the first time that Fred was his father.

"Oh, Frank!" Mattie said when she recognized with whom she was speaking. "How are you? I was wondering if I would ever hear from you again. You don't sound the same as I remember."

"I had a health issue a couple of weeks ago, Mrs. Meyers, and I am just getting back to being able to talk," said Frank. "I am still very sore."

"What happened, Frank?" Mattie sounded concerned.

"I was in a restaurant with some friends two weeks ago, and I had a pretty bad allergic reaction to something I ate," Frank replied. "It was pretty bad, actually. Paramedics had to be called. My tongue had swollen up so I could not breathe, so they had to do an emergency tracheotomy, right there in the restaurant."

Mattie, taken aback by the severity, said, "Oh my goodness, Frank. What did you have that triggered the reaction?" Frank noted that she seemed to understand exactly what he was saying.

Frank replied, "I am fairly sure it was butter that was used in the seafood dish I was eating. Up until that incident, I normally did not have a major problem with small amounts of butter. I've never had a reaction that severe."

"That's right. You said you were allergic to milk when you and Gayle visited. That's something we have in common, you know," said Mattie.

"That's exactly what made me call you today, Mrs. Meyers. When I was at the hospital, a doctor asked if anyone in my family was lactose intolerant. I first said no, and then thought about you."

Mattie laughed. "So, it wasn't until you were nearly dead that you decided that this old Black woman is your Aunt Mattie?" She stopped laughing and continued on to say, "Frank, I have had severe allergies since I was a child. Milk is just one thing I am allergic to."

Mattie became serious. "My mother, I guess that's your grandmother, had allergies that would break her out horribly. She said she had eczema, but she would get a terrible reaction mostly from chemicals. However, one of her uncles nearly died when he was a baby. His mother learned to avoid feeding him milk. I really don't know how that worked as he got older.

"I've read that *tolerance* to milk evolved mostly in Europeans and is believed to coincide with the domestication of bovines in Asia Minor, and the resulting heavy diets of cow's milk products. Many non-Europeans tend to have some level of intolerance, especially as infants and children. I wouldn't read too much into that, Frank."

Frank asked, "Have you ever had a reaction like I had last week?"

"Lord yes, Frank. Many times," Mattie answered. "I don't think I would have lived to learn how to cope with it if it wasn't for Dr. Meyers, my former husband.

"I remember at my oldest son's six-year-old birthday party, I made the mistake of eating a bowl of ice cream. About thirty minutes later, my body became inflamed with massive red, itching welts from head to toe, both inside and out. As I took off all my clothes, my severe, laborious breathing worsened. I believed death was imminent, Frank. Luckily, my husband had his medical bag in the car and was able to give me a shot of epinephrine, and likely saved my life."

She thought for a moment. "I remember when it was happening, thinking that my husband would not be able to make the distance of one hundred feet to the car to get his medical bag and back in time to give me the injection. Well, of course, he did because I am telling you the story now." She laughed.

Frank commented, "That's *exactly* what I thought at the restaurant, Mrs. Meyers. My entire throat closed. I could not take a single breath. If my best friend's wife was not an anesthesiologist, I think I would have died right there in the restaurant. She laid me out and did a tracheotomy right there. Oh, it hurt *really* bad."

"I would think that it did," Mattie replied. "At the time, I naively associated the severe, life-threatening reaction only with eating ice cream when it was actually milk-related products. Over the years, it got worse. I've found I get a reaction from a number of things that don't even appear to be related."

Frank asked, "So what do you do, Mrs. Meyers?"

"I avoid just about everything that I think even has a remote chance of making me sick. You know, a lot of doctors don't even believe it, Frank. Many people think there is something psychological. Don't believe that Frank."

Mattie continued, "You're probably going to have to learn how to prepare a lot of foods from scratch and freeze them or something. You see, you're about to find out how many processed foods have ingredients that are derived from milk. Hopefully, that's the extent of your sensitivity."

"Well, the food that you made at your house when I was there was pretty tasty, Mrs. Meyers. You made some 'greens,' I think. So yesterday, I went to the store and bought some collard greens. I didn't know what kind to get." Frank laughed. "They were horrible. Nothing like what you made."

Mattie started laughing. "Greens are a southern dish. The trick to making greens is to season them well, use flavor from some kind of fatty meat if your diet allows. Be careful there or you will take away the health benefit with all the fat. I don't use pork because of my religion. I use some chicken broth. Then you have to overcook them!

"If you don't overcook them, they will be tough, bitter, and just plain horrible," said Mattie.

"Oh," Frank replied with a laugh. "I guess that's what I did wrong."

For the next thirty or so minutes, Frank and Mattie talked about cooking. Toward the end of the conversation, Mattie asked, "Did you talk with your mother when you got back, Frank?"

"You mean about Fred?"

"Of course, I mean about Fred." Mattie was silent.

Frank answered, "Fred is my father."

"Okay. Well, you can call me Aunt Mattie and drop all that Mrs. Meyers stuff." She started laughing. "There is no need to make me feel any older than I already am, Frank."

For the next few months, Frank talked to his new Aunt Mattie once or twice a week. At first, they would mostly talk about cooking and avoiding foods of which they were both allergic. However, they also started talking about the family and Frank's father.

A funny thing happened. The more Frank talked with Mattie, the more he realized how much he liked her. He also liked hearing the stories about the Burton family. He found he was warming up quite a bit to this interesting heritage.

During one conversation, Mattie was telling Frank how his mother had taught her siblings, and in fact her grandchildren to be careful when interacting with white people. She said, "Frank, my mother would tell us to always get a receipt when you buy something at a store, no matter how small the purchase.

"She told us a story about a young man who bought a pack of chewing gum and did not get a receipt, and the same white man who sold him the gum accused the man of stealing the gum, Frank," she said. "Do you know that man went to prison for years, simply because he could not show a five-cents receipt to the judge?"

"So," as Frank concluded, "your mother was a little prejudiced."

"No, Frank, I don't think so, at least not in the way I think you mean. Mama did not hate anyone." Mattie added, "How could she? She grew up with warm stories about her grandfather who was white, a former slave owner who by the way Mama heard it, loved all his children white and black. You see, Frank, she never personally knew her grandfather because he died about a year before she was born.

"And Mama, her brothers and sisters knew their stepbrothers and stepsisters," she explained. "They lived in Society Hill, a small South Carolina town, and they all grew up playing together and knowing each other. No, Frank, Mama would say that she hated greed that she said infected some of her grandfather's white children.

"Mama was raised as a God-loving woman and felt that only good came from the Lord, and bad things like greed were part of the Devil's domain. Mama loved to tell the Bible's story about Lazarus being denied the crumbs that fell to the floor from the rich man's table in the book of Luke, Frank."

Frank would just listen. They would talk about everything, family, politics, religion, anything and everything. The more he heard, the more he was fascinated about his new family, especially their history.

That is not to take away from the history of his mother's family. Their family went back four generations into Oregon history, migrating into Oregon in the 1850s along the Oregon Trail in wagon trains. When he combined his overall history, Frank really liked his entire family history. He thought he might even write a book someday.

On his next trip to California, Frank flew himself to a site visit in the Monterey area. The instrument rating that he got the year before made it practical to fly the Mooney on his site trips. It also made it practical for him to take a detour to Fresno on his way back home.

It was July, and when Frank left Monterey a little after eleven that Thursday morning, it was 75 degrees and overcast, a typical summer morning on the central California coast. When he landed in Fresno around noon, it was clear and about 102, a typical summer afternoon for Fresno, not even a hundred miles inland.

For some reason, the hot day did not seem to bother Frank as much, because he was looking forward to sitting down with Mattie. He took a short taxi ride to her home, and the two of them sat down in her kitchen office.

They mostly talked about cooking and dealing with their mutually shared allergies. However, as the afternoon wore on, Frank started talking about what was again weighing on his mind.

"Aunt Mattie, I am having a tough time understanding exactly who I am. I mean, I accepted the facts a long time ago, but it still does not make a lot of sense."

"I don't know what you mean, Frank," Mattie replied. "You know you are Frank Malloy, right? You want to change your name or something?"

"That's one thing that's crossed my mind. But the only people who know anything about my relationship to your side of the family are my mother and David, and I would imagine his wife."

"And you think by changing your name to Burton, something magical is going to happen?" Mattie spoke the last question rhetorically that she immediately answered. "Trust me. You'll still be the same Frank Malloy."

"My former husband used to say, you can take a plum and plant it, water it, fertilize it, take wonderful care of it, read to it, you can even graft it onto another tree, and at the end of the day, what you have is a plum tree." She laughed. "Just like that plum, you are who you are, Frank, even if you attach some other label."

Frank was also laughing as he visualized a bin full of plums at the supermarket, each plum with a little oval label with the words "Burton Plum" stuck on its skin. It might cost more, but it is still just a plum.

Frank was trying to stop laughing. "I see your point very clearly, Aunt Mattie."

Mattie continued to talk. "Like I told you when you were here before, that information about our family does not change you. What changes is what you do with it. And what you do with it is up to you."

"That's an interesting way to look at it," said Frank. "A few days ago, my girlfriend and I were having a discussion about why it seems that people tend to stay in the same class in which they were born. You know, rich people tend to stay rich, and the poor tend to stay poor, no matter how smart they are.

"She used the phrase 'range of normalcy' to describe the limits that people tend to see themselves in what they believe to be normal within the scope of their individual life experiences. If by mere fate, you are born into a family living at the bottom of the economic ladder in the poorest nation on Earth, you see your day-to-day experience as just normal, not necessarily good or bad.

"She believes it is difficult for people to see their lives beyond or below what they believe is the extent of what they see as normal. People born rich, can't see themselves below what they think of as normal for them, and conversely, people that are born poor find it difficult to see beyond their upper limit of normal."

Frank concluded his statement, "My recent experiences make me think that observation goes beyond how we see ourselves economically. I think our entire point of view is within the same scope of our range of normalcy. It is difficult for me or anyone else for that matter that is born and raised as a middle-class white American, to see events outside of that scope. Don't ever have to, and don't want to."

"Don't take this the wrong way, Frank," replied Mattie, "but you just described what is referred to as 'White Privilege.'"

There were a few seconds of silence as both thought about what Mattie and Frank had just discussed. Then Frank again started talking. "A few days after I first met you, I went home to visit my mom and ran into one of my best friends going back to when I was elementary school. Aunt Mattie, he is a racist activist, a skinhead Nazi. That is literal. Now the fact is that Ben has had a tough life, but the point is I cannot just dump him. He was my best friend!"

Mattie looked almost angry when she replied, "From my view, Frank, you should dump him, and anyone like him. Good riddance. The Lord knows we have enough people hating everyone." Then she thought a moment.

"But a Bible verse just popped into my mind, Frank," Mattie added. "'Oh, let your light so shine before men that they may see your good works, and glorify our Father in Heaven.'"

Mattie commented, "It means that we lead by example. It means that we demonstrate to others our innate goodness from God by how we conduct ourselves in our daily lives.

"Frank, we don't get to pick and choose the life we are born into. Only the Lord does, and for His reasons. What we do have are choices, and choices that alter the lives that we affect. Lives, like the lives of our children, or even lives like your friend, if that is what you want to call him. We get to alter the stage in our lives by how we live it. That's how you influence the limits of what your girlfriend calls the range of normalcy."

She continued, "It may very well be that this circumstance of yours was set by God to affect your friend's choices, although I still think you should drop him like a hot potato. Only He knows His purpose, Frank."

"Please excuse me a bit here if I am not as religiously oriented as you, Aunt Mattie. I am not sure if I believe that God has a plan for me in all of this," Frank responded.

Mattie laughed. "That may not be important, Frank. The Lord may very well have a plan for you. That's the important thing. The only things you get are your own choices."

"Choices, you say?" replied Frank.

"Let's say, you decide, you choose, to tell your friend about your father. Who knows? He might have been pondering his mixed-up values for some time, and what you tell him is definitely going to force him to make a decision," Mattie said.

"He's going to have to make a decision, Frank. He's going to have to decide if what he says he believes in, if this hatred that he displays is more important than the relationship, if his friendship with you is more important.

"Have no illusions, Frank. In that example, your friend is probably so ingrained with his views that it is very unlikely that he will choose you. But he might. I've seen stranger things happen. Who knows? Maybe he makes the choice that the Lord wants him to make. In which case there is nothing you can do, because the Lord will make sure that this man gets that choice presented."

She finished with a laugh. "That's what I mean when I said it may not be important what you think about the Lord's plans."

Frank also laughed. "Well, we'll see about the Lord's plans, Aunt Mattie. Right now, my plan calls for me to get to the airport. I want to be very close, if not on the ground in Portland before sunset. I don't like flying over remote mountain areas at night in a single-engine airplane."

"I think you are a bit crazy to be flying those little airplanes anywhere at any time. Tell you what, Frank," said Mattie, "I'll give you a ride to the airport."

Mattie reached over into a box and pulled out a book. She wrote into the book she had authored, "*Welcome to the family, Frank Malloy. May you find what I have written about our family provides the basis for many blessings to come,*" and then signed, "*Aunt Mattie.*" She handed it to Frank.

Frank merely said thank-you as they got up to leave.

Mattie took Frank to the airport. Frank would later say that the scariest part of any airplane trip he had ever taken, was this twenty-minute ride to the airport with his eighty-something Aunt Mattie.

Other than the ride to the airport, Frank's trip home was uneventful, and he indeed got into Portland just before sundown, and arrived at his home about eight o'clock that evening. Barbara was sitting on the sofa reading, having let herself in with her key. Even though they spent most of their off time together, they still maintained separate households.

She said as Frank walked in, "Hi, Frank. How was Monterey?"

Sounding a little distant with his response, he said, "Monterey was fine. Give me a minute and I'll tell you all about my trip." He took his suitcase into the bedroom and then continued talking with his girlfriend.

"Actually, I took a little detour to Fresno," he added when he returned twenty or thirty seconds later.

"Oh... okay. So how was Fresno?" Frank noted the way Barbara replied did not sound like she was the least bit surprised.

Frank sat down on the sofa next to Barbara and gave her a somewhat passionate kiss. He said, "Actually, I need to tell you something that you once said would be a deal breaker. It's important."

Again, to Frank's surprise, Barbara did not seem to be very apprehensive as he made the statement. She simply said, "Go on, Frank."

"I did not tell you that I had found my father. I found him a couple of years ago. His sister and some of his nieces and nephews live in Fresno. I was visiting with my aunt in Fresno." Frank waited for an expected inquisitive response.

She nonchalantly asked, "So what's the deal breaker, Frank?"

"My father is a Black man," Frank factually stated.

Barbara started laughing. "Frank, I've known all about that since the morning after you stood me up at that retirement dinner, a year or so back."

Frank looked dumbfounded as Barbara continued, "Don't you know that David tells Faye everything? And Faye is my best friend. She made David tell me the whole story the next morning at breakfast before they flew down to pick you up from your mother's."

Still laughing, Barbara continued, "Frank, didn't it occur to you that David was going to have to tell me something really important happened when you stood me up for the retirement dinner? Of course, they told me why you had to visit your mom at the last minute."

David replied, "But I thought you said…"

Barbara cut him off. "Frank, if you are going to bring up that hypothetical conversation, it was just that," Barbara interjected. She laughed again. "I said if it was someone like David Brewer, I might have to think a little. You, even at that time, were way past David Brewer.

"The fact is, Frank, I did think about what you told me for a few days after we had that conversation. I concluded that I was far beyond loving you at that point. At that point, it did not make any difference about what your racial background was because I was already past that. If your mom lived in a trailer, spitting tobacco alongside your 14 toothless adult brothers and pregnant sisters, it would have made no difference to me at that point. I'm in love with Franklin Fred Malloy, or whatever last name you choose to be called.

"You know what, Frank?" She paused for a moment before she spoke. "I don't know why your mother did not stay with your father. But I have to say I understand her decision, especially at the time. I guess I am saying that's something you should not hold against her.

"Like I said, it was not a fast decision on my part. It took me a few days to understand where I was with you. Once I fully realized the depth of our relationship, I just thought we'd just deal with it. I can easily see how someone else might not choose as I did."

Frank asked, "So why didn't you say anything?"

"I thought I'd wait until you wanted to talk about it. I wasn't supposed to know, remember? I had to swear to David and Faye that I'd never mention it until you said something. Besides, the question at the time was if I would *marry* a Black man." She laughed again. "The question really is why you were bringing this up at all?" She slipped into a playful voice, "Were you trying to ask me to marry you in an around-about way, Frank?"

"Oh. So, are you saying you want to get married?" Frank also sounded playful with the change in subject.

"Not if you ask me while we are sitting on the sofa in the same way you'd ask me to meet you for lunch," she chuckled. "But if you said it in public, down on one knee and all, you'd probably get the response you want."

Frank sat up a little. "Well, what about your parents?"

"They'll get over it one way or the other." She started laughing again. "Or, were you thinking about marrying one of them?"

The next day, Friday afternoon, Frank indeed showed up at Barbara's job at the hospital, and in front of the people gathered around a nursing station proposed to Barbara, who indeed said yes.

A few weeks later, Mattie had just returned from one of her book clubs' meetings. She was in two. One was a club that was run out of the major bookstores in town, and the other was a group of former teachers that Mattie had worked with over the years. It was this latter group of mostly women, and almost all African-American women that she was thinking about when she came into her house.

During the meeting, the idea came up for Mattie to do a presentation during the Black History Month celebration in the coming February. Essentially, they wanted Mattie to talk about her book and in her view, what it meant to the local African-American community, especially children and young adults.

Mattie would tell you the reason why she wrote and self-published her book was because she wanted to leave something for her children, and their children after. She would say that she wanted her family to understand and have a record of her life. She wanted them to know how both her family and her personal experiences influenced her life.

So, she was flattered when local interest picked up with her writings the year after she published, selling several hundred copies of *Seven Houses* just around town. She was equally flattered when her book club presented the idea of using her and the book as the basis of their Black History Month program.

Another idea came to Mattie the following week. At the next meeting, Mattie suggested that Frank do the presentation about Mattie and Frank's family, and how Mattie's stories and her book influenced what he went through over the previous two years.

Mattie told the group about how Frank came to know and understand who he is. There were several objections. First, this group wanted to spotlight an African-American. At least one objection contended that Frank was not *a real* African-American, and it was felt that the speaker should be a Black person, not a newbie who just read *Roots* for the first time.

Another objection was the circumstance of her brother's life of passing as a White person for as long as he did, which did not exactly exemplify someone who embraces his African-American heritage. After all, this was Frank's father who spent about half of his life in denial of his blackness.

At the next meeting, Mattie argued, "While it may be true that Frank did not know of his African ancestry until later in his life, the fact is that he is African-American, whether he wants to be or not. By any rule, he is as Black as anyone here.

"My book is about our family. My new nephew is in the unique position to tell the family story as I have in my book, and more important, what it means. He will tell a compelling story about how what he discovered influenced the irreversible choices he made.

"You know, this is not like he just decided to take a walk on the Black side for a while, and then jump back to his White life like that book in the fifties. Once Frank had learned about who he was, he accepted the facts, and became who he is now."

Mattie thought for a moment. "I can see how someone might feel that this circumstance is about getting validation from a White perspective. Maybe it is. The fact is that most of us don't need to hear it all because we know that each of our families have similar unique histories that are often hard to verify, that people—white people—say could not have been."

A woman spoke. "What about your brother? You don't think how he lived his life sends the wrong message to young people, Mattie?"

Mattie's first response was defensive. "My brother Fred was an exceptionally good person. Anyone who knew him will tell you that."

Mattie forced herself to relax a bit and gather her thoughts. "Self-esteem is what this presentation is all about. The contrast between my brother and my nephew's choices graphically illustrates the result. I think young people will clearly see that. "

There was quite a bit more discussion before the meeting broke up. Later that evening, Mattie called Frank, who was working in Arizona. Frank had just had dinner and was watching CNN in his motel room when his cellphone rang.

Seeing the caller ID said it was his aunt, he answered with a nervous giggle, "Hello, Aunt Mattie." He still felt a little strange when he called her Aunt Mattie.

"Hi, Frank. I have something that I'd like you to consider," she replied. "What do you know about Black History Month?"

"Not very much," Frank answered. "I see the things they have on television, and it seems my boss has done some things around town. What month is Black History Month?"

Mattie laughed, and then seriously said, "Frank, that's something that you really need to know about. It's the month of February."

"I don't understand why there needs to be a special month for Black history. There should only be one history for Americans," Frank replied.

Mattie was getting a little exasperated with the conversation. "Frank, you of all people should know why we need to pay a little more attention to African-American history. I remember just a few months ago, you didn't even believe what I was saying was true until you read it for yourself in official documents and on the Internet."

"I know what you're saying, Aunt Mattie. I just think that this is all part of American history and should be taught as part of history, period," replied Frank. "I don't see why there is only one month a year that brings this information into focus."

Mattie broke into near uncontrollable laughter. "I misunderstood. Maybe you've come further than I realized. I was a schoolteacher for thirty years and I agree with you, Frank. But it does not get taught because the teachers don't know, or they don't want people to know about these things.

"That's the fact, Frank. Right now, much of this history is not being taught to any large degree. So, for the moment, Frank, Black History Month is what we've got."

"Okay, Aunt Mattie. What is it that you'd like me to consider? Hope it is not doing a program like David does each year out at the local airport." Frank said that in a joking manner.

"Oh. Your friend David does a Black History Month Program?"

"If that's what you call it. David does a special program with this guy named Jessie Sampson. He was part of the Tuskegee Airmen and flew a P51 Mustang during WWII. He takes some of the local kids up for a ride in his airplane, and then they do a dinner to raise money for aviation-related scholarships. I help giving the airplane rides."

"Your employer sounds like quite a man. I hope to meet him sometime."

"David is great, Aunt Mattie. He takes one or two kids each year and teaches them to fly. He does the same thing here at the office. I started working for David when I was in college as a paid summer intern."

"Well, before we go too far off promoting your boss to the sainthood, let me ask you what you think about doing a presentation for my book club in February?"

"Huh? You mean do a presentation for Black History Month? You gotta be kidding."

"Oh, no, Frank. I am being profoundly serious. I think your story is unique. If done right, it would be very impressive. And from what you tell me about what you do at work, you definitely have the presentation skills."

"Aunt Mattie. I have told exactly three people about my father and our family. Now you want me to come to Fresno and tell a hundred people all about myself."

Mattie chuckled. "More like about three hundred. Look at it as practice, Frank."

"Okay, I'll think about it. There are more people involved in all this than just me."

"I know there is, Frank. No rush. Try to let me know in the next week before my group meets again."

Frank and Mattie talked for a few more minutes before they hung up. *What a mess,* he thought.

He took his phone and selected "Mom" from his contact list, selected her name, and clicked the "Call" button.

"Hi, Mom," Frank said when Cheryl answered.

"Hi, Frank. What's got you calling me in the middle of the week? Are you in Portland?"

"No. I'm in Phoenix until Thursday. I might come down and visit over the weekend."

"Oh, that will be great, Frank." She continued, "So, what's up, Franklin?"

"Mom, I just got off the phone with Mattie Meyers."

"Who?" Cheryl said, sounding a little puzzled, then remembered, "Oh, you mean your new aunt."

"She wants me to be part of a program she is doing for that Black History Month stuff."

There were several seconds of silence before Cheryl replied, "You mean she wants you to stand up in front of a group of people and tell them about Fred and me? That woman has a lot of nerve, Franklin, to ask you to do something like that. That's a bad idea, I think."

Frank was a little surprised by her response. "Really? Why do you think so?"

"I thought you had just let that drop," she replied. "How does this do you any good, Franklin? How does this do anything good for anyone?"

"Mom, I had not let it drop. The fact is that I think about it every day. At some point, I must make some real decisions. I am getting married in less than a year. Barbara and I want to have children, Mom. What do I do… the same things that you and Fred were doing? No, I cannot just let it drop, Mom.

"I am not going to live two lives or try to hide one life from the other. I am not going to be Frank when I am in Fresno and someone else when I come home to Bend, or wherever else my life takes me. Don't you see that's the same reason I was being so hard on the father I never even knew?"

"Franklin, I still think this idea is very bad."

"Mom, I respect your feelings. However, until this moment, I did not realize this is something I am going to have to do. I can no more dodge this than I could ignore the facts about Fred on the day that man showed me his picture. The thing is I need you to be with me on this, Mom."

"I don't think I can, Franklin," his mother answered.

That is where this conversation ended, but the topic was far from resolved.

The other woman in Frank's life, his fiancée Barbara, had no problem with Frank going to Fresno and outing himself. Her thought was that the more out in the open, the simpler life would be for their entire family when they were married.

Thus, a week later when Frank talked to his Aunt Mattie, he agreed to make the presentation. Mattie had many specific tasks to complete. The first was that a specific location and time for the event had to be set, as well as all the physical requirements.

Frank had to gather materials and create a presentation. One of the first things that Frank did was to gather as much factual material as possible. He started by researching the two court cases that Mattie had previously mentioned, and he subsequently found more than a year earlier. This time he read the documents very carefully while making detailed notes.

A few nights later, he went to a genealogy website and began looking for census records to document the existence of the individuals in court documents against what he had learned from his Aunt Mattie. He compared information from what he had learned from speaking with other Meyers family members and concluded that all the information was accurate and consistent.

The last thing Frank did was to reread Mattie's book, this time with an eye for detail, making careful reading notes. When he finished, he put the book down and looked at all the information he had noted. He leaned back in his chair, closed his eyes, and thought.

He started to envision a presentation that told how he came to know his father, and how he came to accept his father's family. Frank imagined pictures choreographed to his presentation. He could visualize telling the audience what Mattie had told him about the Tedder's as he rolled through a collage of old pictures Mattie had in her collection. Frank thought he could even use some audio/video clips with Mattie or Gayle telling one or more of Fred's stories.

To put an exclamation point onto the presentation, Frank thought he should create a small leave behind booklet documenting the family history. Something simple, about 8 letter-sized pages, the first part documenting Fred and his parental family, the center showing a family tree, and the last part documenting the struggles of Fred's grandfather and great-grandfather's family, along with a bibliography. Everything factually documented.

"I am who I am," Frank said aloud. That is a nice title and theme, he thought.

He had to admit that as he thought about how he planned his presentation, he started to warm up to the idea. There was only one other major thing he needed to make this happen.

Frank had to get his mother to sign off. He did not tell anyone that he would not do it if Cheryl did not approve, even if it meant a last-minute cancellation. However, each time he brought the subject up with her was not encouraging.

As the date approached, David and Faye decided they wanted to be part of Frank's presentation. David volunteered to fly his wife and Frank to Fresno because his aviation program that David participated in each year was scheduled on the Saturday, the day before David's program. Barbara who would be in Los Angeles for a continuing education seminar, decided to rent a car and drive to Fresno to join Frank and catch a ride home with David and Faye.

Frank's mother, the only person to whom he had given veto power remained unresolved. And it remained unresolved until just two days before the presentation. On the Friday before the scheduled event, Frank got off work and drove the three hours to Bend. He arrived at his mother's house about seven in the evening.

Frank had one ace in the hole when it came to convincing his mother to sign off. Frank was nearly convinced that his mom would never jeopardize or embarrass Frank for something he thought was of the highest importance. The conversation that ensued went like this.

Frank and his mom sat together in the living area of the home where Frank grew up. Whenever Frank was in the house, he always felt like a child. Everything was nearly exactly as it was when he was growing up. He could remember the day they moved into the home, a few weeks after his great-aunt had died. It even smelled the same.

"Mom, I need you to come with me to Fresno on Sunday." Frank was negotiating. He thought if he asked her to do more she might at least settle and approve what he was going to do.

Cheryl laughed. "Franklin, you know I can't take my Sunday and travel all the way to Fresno, California. I do have a life, and I cannot just change things whenever. Besides, I don't want you to do what you are doing in the first place."

"I need you to tell me why," said Frank.

"Frank, I am your mother. You don't demand that I tell you anything."

"In this case, you do need to explain a bit. You see, what I am going to do on Sunday, what I have committed to do, rests on what you tell me, Mom."

"Well, I don't, Frank. However, I am going to try to tell you why I am so opposed. I have thought about it since all this started over the last two years. I must live here, Franklin. This is still a small town. Most of these people I've known since I was a child.

"I am not ready to be ostracized by all the people here. This is not like a big city where you can live somewhere and your next-door neighbor does not care about their neighbor, the person that lives right across the street. I'd even guessed that the man who I work for might not want me around when he finds out," she concluded.

"I am glad you said when he finds out, because sooner or later he and everyone else you are concerned with are going to know anyway. Mom, I cannot live and perpetuate a lie about who I am. I certainly will not allow my children to grow up and face the same. Your friends are going to find out," Frank explained. "Besides, I thought you told me it was all about me?"

Cheryl thought a moment. "It was about you, Franklin, but at this moment, I have to admit it's all about me."

"Well, you need to consider not just me, but my family that is about to come," Frank replied. "Mom, my children, your grandchildren, are going to know exactly who they are. And they are going to be proud of you. They are also going to be proud of the other blood that flows in their veins."

Frank got up. "Think about it, Mom. I am going to respect what you say, but it is going to happen anyway." He left the room.

Apparently, blood is thicker than mud, because the next morning, Cheryl did something that was somewhat astonishing. On a whim, she called the wife of her church pastor, just to see how badly she would feel if she did not teach her Sunday school class the next morning. She kept asking Cheryl why she could not do it. Finally, a little exasperated with her continued question, Cheryl just told her everything about Frank and Fred.

After she hung up the phone, she sat thinking about what she had done. An admission to the woman to whom she had just spilled her guts was like putting everything onto the front page of the city newspaper. About twenty minutes later Frank came into the kitchen where she was sitting, fully prepared to continue his discussion.

Cheryl looked up and merely asked, "What time are we leaving in the morning?"

# CHAPTER 14

## Family Reunion

The actions that Frank Malloy will do today would lead one to likely describe Frank as either "... his own man who is not afraid to think outside the box," or, "... that crazy white man who wants to be Black." Either way, it is certain that Frank Malloy on this day did at least one thing that was vastly different than he might have done two years earlier.

This story started today, with Frank and his mother, along with David and Faye Brewer, leaving the Bend airport on a cold Sunday morning in February 2012.

They were traveling 500 miles south to Fresno, California, where Frank was scheduled to tell a group of people awaiting him of the events that transpired over the last two years, and what it meant to him.

The last thing he said to his mother before they boarded the airplane was, "This is your last chance, Mom. If you do not want me to do this, say so now."

His mother just nodded and with a blank facial expression said, "Let's go see your family, Frank. Everyone here knows all about it by now."

Frank thought this trip was like going to his coming out party. If he were telling this group he was gay, it would be said he was coming out of the closet. However, what he was about to do was more akin to moving into another house. As Frank saw it, the emotions he felt now were probably about the same.

Normally, Frank and David would have been very chatty over the intercom headsets, talking about flying. This morning, Frank quietly sat in the back of the cabin, seated across from and facing his mother. Faye sat up front with her husband who was flying the airplane.

Although it was quiet, it was an extremely comfortable trip. This was exactly what this new TBM turbine was designed to do. That is, to take four or five adults and their baggage about five hundred miles in pressurized comfort and get them to their destination within a couple of hours. At 28,000 feet, they were above most of the weather, sitting in fully reclining leather seats, with overhead reading lights, and an entertainment center. Each passenger seat had a folding table, and there were even refreshments on-board if they so desired.

However, Frank and his mom had more than their fair share of baggage on this flight. During the one and half hours it took to cover the 500 miles between Bend and Fresno, Frank spent most of his time going through the presentation materials on his notebook computer that he would be using later that day. He would later say that he was looking forward to his presentation, albeit extremely nervous about where the result would take him.

Cheryl spent her time reading Mattie's book that Frank had given to her the night before. The more she read, the better she felt about joining Frank. She could see how her son would want to be a part of the Burton saga. In the final analysis, even Cheryl realized that she and Fred printed the ticket for this plane ride almost thirty years ago.

They landed in Fresno around ten in the morning, and Mattie's youngest son, also named David, was waiting to take them first to have a late breakfast, and then to the location where Mattie's book club was doing their Black History Month program.

After breakfast, they went to the church where the program would take place. It was Mattie's church, a small Seventh-Day Adventist church, not used for a regular Sunday service, in a new building in an older and still predominantly African-American part of town. His Aunt Mattie was already at the church when they arrived.

The program would not start for about two more hours, about two o'clock that afternoon. Frank and David Brewer set up and tested all the audio and visual equipment he would be using. He had done these kinds of things before, although nothing that was this personal.

Barbara arrived from Los Angeles at about one and joined Frank's mother and Faye who were helping Mattie set up to sign books in the church foyer. They spent a lot of time just talking and getting to know Mattie. About half an hour later, people began filling the seats for the program. They were expecting no more than about three hundred people to attend the program.

But as the program was about to start, Frank could see that there were more than twice that number seated in the audience. Frank was a little surprised at the number of Whites that were in the audience and noted a fairly large number of cowboy hats sticking out in the crowd. Apparently, Gayle had personally invited many of Fred's friends she had met at her uncle's funeral.

When the program started, Mattie spoke about ten minutes regarding her book *Seven Houses*, and then described how her experiences and the history of her family came to have a profound impact upon another person. She then introduced Frank as her nephew who took the dais and began to speak to the six hundred or so people gathered in the room.

Frank began his presentation, although he would admit he was a bit nervous. That was not because he was unprepared or inexperienced. Frank developed the presentation over the past few months, and he was a seasoned presenter at conferences and computer seminars for his company.

He started, "I cannot say that I know what it is actually like to be African-American, because it has only been two years since I first discovered my father, and his ethnicity. It has really been just a few months since I actually accepted the fact. And I think just weeks since I have really embraced my newfound family.

"I think the closest analogy might be along the lines of the first time someone really understands their own mortality. Like the day you have a near-death experience, or the doctor tells you that you have an ailment that is going to likely kill you in a short amount of time. At some point after, most will accept this as just another fact about being alive. I understand that because I also had a near-death experience. The point is I now accept death as a fact about the reality of who I am. That reality indeed changed me to some degree."

He took the wireless microphone and now held it as he walked away from the dais and smoothly continued speaking.

"In the same sense, I think that for most Whites, at least for me, the idea of being anything other than White never crosses your mind in any real way, unless something is revealed to you that forces you to realize there is another reality, a privilege in America, associated with being White. And conversely, there is a reality of being non-White in this country."

Gesturing at himself, he said, "The interesting thing is that each day I wake up, I still find that I am Frank Malloy. I still like my work. I still love flying airplanes. I still love strawberry pie, and I still like holding the door for senior women. I do find myself questioning the rationale for many of the decisions I have made in the past.

"In some cases, I ask myself if I did certain things, or made decisions, in a careless manner because I simply would not allow myself to see things through the prism of someone else's eyes."

He walked over and pointed to Mattie. "I was fortunate, or as both my new Aunt Mattie and my mother would tell me, I was blessed by God, to have found a family that had at least one extraordinary family member, my Aunt Mattie. She was willing to talk with me about from where I came and was open to help me as I was struggling to interpret what this meant.

"I was equally blessed to have one incredibly good friend, maybe my very best friend, David Brewer, who is African-American, and like Aunt Mattie, was willing to help me understand what this meant. Without them I might still be wallowing around in a state of denial." He nodded at David, who signaled to lower the lights.

The young picture of Fred, the same picture that Frank first saw two years earlier, appeared on the screen behind him in the darkened room as Frank spoke.

"This is the man I first met two years ago, although I did not meet him personally, I met him through the legacy of both him and his family. This man is my father." As Frank spoke, the pictures on the screen rotated through several black-and-white childhood photographs of Fred, and then a color picture of Fred taken in the years before he died.

Frank continued with his presentation. "The process of accepting my father was not easy. I think the hardest thing for me was dealing with how what I discovered about who I am, would affect the lives of those I love. Ironically, both my mother and my fiancée, as they either stated or demonstrated by their actions, first believed it was more beneficial from their perspective to keep such things hidden. But after some reflection, they both came to understand the importance of being frank and earnest. Both are sitting in the audience hearing me tell you who I am, and from where I came."

The screen dissolved into the old photograph that Mattie first showed to Frank of the Tedder family outside of their home in Society Hill, South Carolina, as Frank spoke.

"My Aunt Mattie, through both her words and the history she describes in her book, told me about my family's history, a history that will make anyone proud. It started with the mother and father of this man. This man was the son of a former Black slave woman named Adline, and a former White slave owner named William."

Frank waved at the pictures on the screen and continued, "This is a photograph of my great-grandfather, James Tedder, who my Aunt Mattie knew as 'Grandpa Jim' as a child, and who was the son of the former White slave owner William Tedder and his wife, my great-great grandmother, Adline Tedder, William's former slave.

"From my research, I determined they were indeed married after the Civil War through both common-law, and legal ceremony. I am so proud of the extraordinary steps Adline and William took to secure the welfare of their nine children." The screen zoomed into a close view of James Tedder as Frank told the story of his family.

Turning back to the audience, Frank went on to say, "But William and Adline's efforts were in vain. In vain because of three hundred years of racial attitudes that supported an economy based on slavery that had permeated into every fiber of the South Carolina legal system.

"I believe that those same intrinsic racial attitudes as my father, Fred Langston Burton, learned through actual experience in his young years as a runaway on his own in the deep South, were the source of my father's denial of our outstanding family. He learned to do what he felt he had to in order to survive in a racially prejudiced world. Let me tell you the facts about my family and my father."

For the next forty-five minutes, Frank presented his family's history in chronological order, using old photographs, maps, historical documents, and even video clips he took of his Aunt Mattie describing events and stories that were part of that history. He told the story of his father's life and experiences.

As the lights came back up, Frank was speaking from the lectern. "I have learned a number of things over the last two years. As a White man, I came to realize that there really is something that we now refer to as 'White Privilege' in this country. To me it meant that I never had to look at anything from any other point of view, because the alternative view had no effect on my day-to-day life. I never had to examine anything from another perspective until I woke up one morning and realized I was not White.

"When that cloak of privilege was removed, the filter of irrelevancy was also removed. Thus, without that filter of White Privilege, I now see how the denials of the privileged ignore things like racially condoned police brutality because the police are doing just what the privileged want when it comes to the irrational fear and suspicion of young Black men.

"Without the cloak, my eyes do not automatically roll when someone makes mention that the country owes African-Americans for hundreds of years of the cruelest exploitation under the eyes of God. Maybe reparations of some kind are something we need to consider in some form to finally address the racism that is woven into the very fabric of our flag and country."

Shaking his head, Frank said in a low thoughtful voice, "I must admit that I am not comfortable with the option of making the decision every day if I want to wear my blackness. That's why I concluded that I must decide exactly who and what I am.

"At the very least, I am something of 'Mixed Race.' Nevertheless, as I have learned, mixed race with just one drop of Black blood, even today, is still African-American. Why would I have struggled so much with how to deal with it if that were not the case? If you had asked me two years ago, that's how I would have described someone with my ancestral heritage.

"So as a Black man, I can see from this perspective how important it is to keep history as documented as possible. Many facets of the story I just told, by many, would be swept under the rug in disbelief. It is only through this preservation that we understand our legacy, pretty and not so pretty. That's why books such as Aunt Mattie's *Seven Houses* are so important. That's why Black History Month is so important. That's something I would not have realized from my prior perspective.

"I am thrilled to be living at this very moment in history. We are two years into living in a United States with its first non-White president. Like many of you, my Aunt Mattie will tell you that she is amazed to be living to see it. I can see through my short life experiences that there will be drawbacks in the future. It will not surprise me if the antithesis of our current President emerges in the next election or two. I wonder how we will resolve this conflict, this struggle for our nation's identity.

"Most of all, I am amazed. I am amazed at the plan my God has allowed me just a small role. I just hope that the choices I make are consistent with His will.

"We don't get to pick the framework in which we are born. Only God decides such things. When I woke up this morning, do you know whom I saw in the mirror? I was the total of everything about my mother, my father and me. I was the total of all my experiences and dreams. But my final thought was that I am Franklin Fred Malloy-Burton, the same person I was the day before, and every day since my birth. I now just see the world from another point of view, a view I considered irrelevant until I got to know my family."

Frank received a standing ovation. After the program ended, he sat between his Aunt Mattie and his mother, as Mattie signed books in the church foyer. Just about everyone seeking an autograph asked Frank to write something into their copy.

Quite a few people stopped and talked to Frank, both Black and White. Many told Frank that they knew his father Fred, and how much of a close friend he was. They told him how much it meant to hear Frank tell of his own journey.

One person walked up to the table and held out his copy for Frank to sign. As Frank looked up, he recognized him to be John Assorian, the man who Frank had met two years earlier and started Fred down this road. John said, "See, Frank, I told you that there might be some good things about finding out about your father."

Instantly, a broad smile appeared on Frank's face. "Hello, John. I am sure glad you came out today." Frank chuckled. "I absolutely would not be here if I had not met you."

Frank stood up and shook John's hand. Then John said, "I also want you to meet my wife Asia. She would not let me come out the house unless I brought her too."

Asia looked at her husband with an exasperated look, and then spoke to Frank. "Don't believe what John tells you, Frank. That's why he ends up sleeping on the couch so often." She laughed.

Then Asia added, "I knew you father very well. I think Fred would have been very proud to hear his son speak so highly about him and his family. I think he would have liked you, Frank."

It took a little less than an hour for the church to clear out. By five-thirty, they were back aboard the Big Airplane headed back to Bend and Portland. David dropped off Frank and his mom in Bend, and continued home with Faye and Barbara. Once sitting at the little desk where he had spent so much time while growing up studying reading, writing, math, science, and history, Frank thought about his own history. He thought about what it meant in his life.

Frank took out his cellphone and found the contact entry for Ben Reynolds. He thought a moment, and then clicked the "Call" button.

Ben answered with surprise, "Hello. Frank?"

"I know it's late, Ben," said Frank, who then added, "I love you like a brother. You know that, right?"

"Yeah, Frank, of course I do. Me too," replied Ben. "What's this all about, buddy?"

Then Frank said, "I want to talk with you for a few minutes about some things that are going to change either you or me, maybe both. I am going to tell you some things about myself that you don't know." Frank paused. "I am who I am. And who I am is…" He was frank and earnest.

And Frank was amazed.

# EPILOGUE

*"This above all: to thine own self be true,*
*And it must follow, as the night the day,*
*Thou canst not then be false to any man.*
*Farewell, my blessing season this in thee!"*

*Hamlet Act 1, scene 3, 78–82*

# FRANK'S RESEARCH

## *Conclusions*

For several months following Frank's Black History Month presentation in Fresno, he received many emails and other correspondences asking questions about the way he presented his material. What follows is how he responded.

Many people questioned if the events he described immediately after slavery were fact, or just matriculated stories. Frank received many emails and letters asking him about the validity of William and Adline's life, and their relationships to their children and William's White family. He directed them to the two court cases of "*Moody v. Tedder*" and "*Tedder v. Tedder,*" using the same search methodology previously described in the chapter "Frank's Research: The Tedders."

One email asked Frank why he illustrated a slice of both Adline and William's life in the manner he presented, similar to what is depicted in chapters one and two.

Frank wrote, "In order to understand why I presented the thoughts and interactions between the Tedders in the manner I did, I looked at what was occurring in South Carolina history during this period in American history. My presentation's dialog is based upon what I understood was happening in history at the end of the Civil War.

"According to all information available about Adline Tedder, she was born into slavery in either 1840 or 1844. Tedder v. Tedder states that Adline was the personal property of Jimima Tedder, William Tedder's first wife before William and Jimima were married. There was no evidence of Jimima having a prolonged illness, nor is there any evidence to support the idea that William and Adline were in any kind of sexual relationship prior to 1867."

Frank goes on to say the census records from 1880 set Augustus' year of conception, the oldest of William and Adline's children, as early as late 1867. This conclusion is extrapolated from his age at the time the census was taken. Frank felt it was plausible that William and Adline could have begun a sexual relationship sometime prior to 1867. The facts say that a marital relationship may have started as early as 1867, but no later than 1875. Tedder v. Tedder states:

*"James Moody once lived in the house with the old man, and Adline (sic) did not then live there. After Moody moved out Adline (sic) moved in and lived there until her death. On the cross-examination by the defendants, the witness testified as follows:*

**Q:** *"I understand you to say she lived there right straight on until she died?"*
**A:** *"She did."*
**Q:** *"You mean she continued to live in the house there with the old man just as husband and wife would live up to the time of death?"*
**A:** *"Yes sir."*

Adline died in 1890. Frank explained that the latest date that Adline and William could have set up housekeeping was no later than 1875 according to the information elucidated in Moody v. Tedder. This is the year the court record states that Mahalie Moody and her husband—believed to be James Moody—started keeping their own land. As stated in "Moody v. Tedder":

*"... Plaintiff, Mahalie Moody, and husband, went on the land in 1875, and instituted this proceeding against her father and brothers..."*

"The key point is William Tedder's White children were definitely out of his home by 1875. I chose the date of 1867, the earliest year of Augustus' conception, to be the date that Adline and William began living together as husband and wife. The cohabitation date of sometime after 1870 is equally possible, if one considers that the 1870 census lists family members for William Tedder to be his White children. It could just as well be that William maintained both his White and Black families until 1875, circumstances that I learned were not uncommon during and after slavery," wrote Frank.

Regardless of the year, Frank said he could see how Adline could not help but be amazed when she found herself in a marital relationship with her former master. She would have had to be in amazement every day when contrasting her life in slavery against her new life with William Tedder.

The extrapolation of census data after the Civil War begs for an answer to a key question. Why would William Tedder, a 42 year old White man, after successfully raising a completely free White family, begin a second family with a former slave? The answer to that question may have been as simple as playing the odds for his own self-preservation. That is why I stated in my presentation (as written in Chapter 2):

"... William would acknowledge that one of the main reasons he decided to start a family with Adline, and live with her as his wife had a lot to do with hanging onto his farm and business interest, in what he saw as the wave of possible reality in post-Civil War South Carolina..."

William was by far no saint when it came down to slavery. For nearly ten years, between 1856 and the end of the Civil War, William managed and traded in slaves with the skill of the southern businessperson he was. Moody v. Tedder states that the way William skillfully saved the farm was through the sale of three slaves in 1859. Frank wrote that he believed that initially, William was probably just looking out for himself.

"Immediately following the Civil War, the political winds at the time could be described as light winds blowing out of the north, with occasional strong gusts from the south," Frank wrote.

Following the assassination of Abraham Lincoln, Vice President Andrew Johnson succeeded Lincoln into the White House. Johnson was a compromise Vice-Presidential candidate for the anti-slavery Republican Party, coming from a "border" state to politically appeal to voters in Union states that may have a little more sympathy with the former Confederate secessionist, and hopefully, vote for the Lincoln-Johnson presidential ticket. Remember, Lincoln was not a shoo-in for reelection in 1864. For apparent good reason, mainline Republicans of the time viewed Johnson with suspicion.

The presidential vetoes by Johnson of several key pieces of post-Civil War congressional legislation, the Civil Rights Bill of 1866, and the Reconstruction Acts of 1867 were all overridden by Congress, and outlined the sharp differences between Republicans and Andrew Johnson, so much so that these differences led to this nation's first presidential impeachment proceeding.

Although the Civil War began off the coast at Fort Sumter, for the most part, South Carolina missed a great deal of that war's destruction, if you make the exception of the Union's unsuccessful assault upon the harbor city of Charleston. However, in 1865, after completing his March to the Sea, General William Tecumseh Sherman indeed marched north from Savannah, Georgia, across South Carolina, burning the city of Columbus, and numerous towns and farms along the way.

We do know that Sherman at Columbus was within about 80 miles as the crow flies from Society Hill, but there is no direct evidence to support that he or any other military operation directly affected the Tedder Farm as cited in the story but could have.

Although Moody v. Tedder mentions that there was theft and vandalism at the Tedder farm during the Civil War, it makes no mention of possible perpetrators. At the very least, indirect consequences would have affected William Tedder's thinking and his farm operation.

One of those effects that would have likely had an impact on William Tedder's decision-making was the policy of Federal troops turning over land and farming operations to the former slaves after the war's end. Furthermore, in 1868, the new constitution in South Carolina provided access for former slaves into the South Carolina political system. Initially African-Americans filled as many as 76 of the 124 seats of the South Carolina legislature.

Thus, a person in William Tedder's position might have considered finding the best place to hang his hat for future security. On one hand, there was a group of those that would continue to fight a war of terrorism to keep some semblance of slavery forever, by just about any means necessary. On the other, there were those that appear to have included William Tedder, who felt it was in everyone's best interest to accept the emerging new way of doing things that included a degree of assimilation of African-Americans into the American system.

Any way you slice it up, it appears that William made a conscious decision to go with what he saw as the wave of the future and orient his life after the war based on the current prevailing winds of legitimate post-war change. From a practical perspective, this was a win-win scenario. In any political outcome, William would have on his own, or through marriage, kept his land and his livelihood.

Frank continued, "There is one other possible dynamic that I suggested in my presentation. William and Adline were carrying on a relationship before the war ended, maybe even before the Civil War even began. In 1859, Adline would have been no younger than 15 years old, and as the property of William, been easy pickings for a thirty- or forty-something-year-old man with complete control of Adline's life. In my presentation, I chose that possibility in my imagined tale of William and Adline's relationship, even though there is no direct evidence that this was the actual basis of their relationship."

For whatever reasons William chose the path he took with Adline, things seemed to work out in William's favor in the few years immediately following the Civil War. During the first four or five years following the war, the country as a rule was in a mood to change the South and enforced the will of the country onto the southern states in general.

However, gradually, interest in reconstruction started down a slow road to irrelevancy as far as the rest of the country was concerned and was an obsolete issue by 1878. In that year, the climate had shifted to a strong sustained wind coming out of the old South. The major change occurred during the Presidential election of Rutherford Hayes.

From the time Andrew Johnson took office following Abraham Lincoln, the number of Federal troops that were left to enforce United States and local laws dwindles in number from year to year during both the Johnson and Ulysses S. Grant administrations.

As a result of a compromise designed to ensure the election of Hayes during a time that the American economy was in a downturn, the country had lost much of its zeal for unmitigated former slave assimilation, and most Americans apparently felt the country could not afford to support enforcement of Reconstruction in the present economic situation. Consequently, they struck a deal that completely removed the remaining federal troops in the South, including South Carolina.

"As I stated in my fictional dialog of William Tedder, from the end of the Civil War there had always been an undercurrent to somehow maintain some semblance of the old slave system. The Union in 1865 rejected South Carolina's first attempt at a post-Civil War constitution, as unacceptable for reinstatement into the Union. Essentially, this unsuccessful constitution had a list of new laws that would have kept the old slave system intact, except for the little part about being called a slave," wrote Frank.

Frank explained that the constitution that was finally accepted, and that allowed South Carolina to rejoin the Union as a state, was in 1868. This new constitution assimilated former slaves into the political system.

However, a percentage of southerners never embraced this new way of doing things. Almost immediately, many secret and illegal groups began to emerge that essentially terrorized the former slaves to keep them out of the political-economic system... it worked.

Frank replied to one email, "Looking at the end of Confederacy from today's perspective, I see today's racial issues are evidence that it would have been more beneficial if the former citizens and the Confederate States of America were treated more harshly, just as we would treat any defeated country at the end of a bloody war. By allowing Federal enforcement of anti-slavery laws to disappear and later allow the emergence of local laws designed to keep the former slaves in a subservient role, this environment created the path leading to today's racial problems.

"The trend to promote the former leaders of the Confederacy as American heroes through statues, monuments and even within education after about 1880 I believe is why we still have issues of racism at the level we have today," wrote Frank.

"Court decisions after 1880 such as Dred Scott and more cases such as the 1917 South Carolina Tedder v. Tedder decisions when looked at in totality all cemented racially motivated legal positions detrimental to African-Americans in a systemic fashion," explained Frank.

Frank said, "This is the reason why I created a dialog between William and his Black children." Frank's presentation used these words by William telling his children:

"...Them days of Union enforcin' the law is long past, and we are in dangerous times, boys..."

Then William goes on to express a warning to his Black children, and of course later starts doing things to protect his children.

However, the fact is that the intimidation worked. It worked especially after 1878 because these groups functioned unchecked by the Federal government. So, by the 1880s, any vestiges of political assimilation of former slaves were completely wiped out, replaced by laws that pretty much guaranteed they would be in a subservient position for an exceedingly long time.

These actions were the predecessor for the infamous Dred Scott decision in the 1890s by the United States Supreme Court that cemented this system into United States law for the next half-century or more.

Frank concluded his email by saying, "The fictitious interactions I created between the Tedders and the thought processes I describe are based on this historical setting, along with the factual information of the Tedders."

There is only one catch. Although what Frank said about the facts regarding the Tedders and the story's rationale are factually true, Frank Malloy himself never existed.

That of course means that none of his immediate family or friends from Bend, Oregon, ever existed. His associates in Portland, including David and Faye Brewer, as well as John and Asia Assorian, are also purely fictitious people.

However, Mattie B. Meyers and her family—my family—including the Burtons and Tedders, really existed, mostly as described in Frank's story.

# Author's Notes

Thus, the story you just read is mostly fiction. However, the basis of many of my characters are real, actual people whose identities are unchanged in the book. I, David K. Meyers, the author, created the fictitious characters to tell the true story elements about the Meyers, Burton, and Tedder families with relevance.

I have read of sculptors who say that the image was always in the medium they were working, be it a log, a stone, or a chunk of clay. It had the image already present in its raw mass. All the artist had to do was to remove the extra material—the overburden—to clearly reveal the image.

Similarly, the story I revealed was present in the court cases, my mother's memoirs, the photos, and the stories that have existed in our family for generations. All I had to do was remove the irrelevant material to reveal the story that was begging to be exposed. Well, that plus taking a little literary creative liberty.

With creative liberty in mind, although the general premise of my Uncle Fred living two separate lives is true, exactly what life experiences of his were responsible for him adopting his alias life are unknown. However, the incidents cited in my story are what he told in bits and pieces.

I filled in those incomplete gaps based on what could have occurred while imagining what a young Black boy, and later young man, may have witnessed out on his own during and just after the Great Depression in the South. The Fred Langston Burton I knew was an outstanding man that likely just got caught up with what he had learned to say in order to survive in harsh conditions.

I want to also remind readers who may consider this content as mere relics of ancient history, that the events in this book are not ancient at all. I knew my grandmother Julia Tedder-Burton, the oldest daughter of James Tedder, who missed knowing her grandfather by just one year.

My point is there is a contemporary conduit that goes directly back to the birth of her grandfather, William Tedder, in 1821. Remember, America is still a young country with a history that is still being written as you are reading this book.

I wish I could say that I am so witty along with my command of the English language that I came up with the book's title, "To Be Frank and Ernest." The fact is that I gleaned the title from the dialog of Samuel L. Jackson in the 1996 movie *The Long Kiss Goodnight*. I believe there is also a comic strip with a similar name, that plays on the words in a similar manner.

I do like the idea that Frank Malloy turns out to be both frank and earnest!

David K. Meyers

# BIBLIOGRAPHY

"Meyers – Burton Family Tree Branching Up... From Deep Roots" – **Sharon Revis Green** Available from Blurb – www.blurb.com

**"Meyers Family History"** – **Eric Meyers** Available from Blurb – www.blurb.com

**"Moody v. Tedder" Reports of cases heard and determined by the Supreme Court of South Carolina – Pages 557-566** by South Carolina. Supreme Court; Richardson, J. S. G., reporter; Shand, Robert Wallace, 1840-1915, reporter; Etird, Cyprian Melanchthon, 1856- [from old catalog] reporter; Townsend, William Hay, 1868- [from old catalog] reporter; Ray, Duncan C., reporter; Shand, William Munro, 1881- [from old catalog] reporter

**"Seven Houses" by Mattie B. Meyers – Copyright 2010** Available from Blurb – www.blurb.com

**"Tedder v. Tedder" 93 S.E. 19 (S.C. 1917) Supreme Court of South Carolina** As printed at the CourtListener – www.courtlistener.com

**United States Census and Other Birth/Death Data from:**
Acestory.com
GenealogyBank.com

9 781636 614021